Queer Monologues

&

Short Plays

By

Yvonne Hernández

P.O. Box 841
Tobyhanna, PA 18466
(973) 348-5067
sspublishingcompany@gmail.com
www.sharsheypublishingcompany.com

Copyright © 2017 Yvonne Hernàndez
ISBN 13: 978-0-9997922-0-9
ISBN 10: 0-9997922-0-2
Publisher: Shar- Shey Publishing Company LLC
Book Cover Designed by: Dynasty's Visionary Designs
Edited by: ATW Editing

TABLE OF CONTENTS

DEDICATION

To my Uncle Chico: You were the only person in my youth who inspired me, encouraged me, had faith in me, never gave up on me, loved me unconditionally, and always made me feel special. I am forever grateful, and I will love you always. If I am chosen to see you in heaven, then I will know that death will be worth living.

INTRODUCTION

I spent many years locked in the closet. Afraid. I knew what I felt and exactly who I was. Yet I denied it. I wanted to. I had to. All I had ever heard about Lesbians was that they are "Sucia" – dirty. Una "Maricona." *Maricona.* A derogatory and degrading word that, believe me, was very difficult to say. In Spanish it is considered the 'M' word and I was not like that, so I buried it. Denied it.

I met a good man and I got married because I felt this would cure me of this thing called homosexuality. I had two beautiful boys. I love them so. I was scared. Would they still love me if they knew their mother was like that once upon a time? Would they be ashamed?

My boys eventually did what all children do. They grew up, spread their wings, and left me for a place called college. A place called life. I was alone. When I finally picked myself up from my empty nest syndrome, I decided to spoil myself with a little trip.

I was on the beach in Sanibel Florida. I couldn't take my eyes off the lovely women. I tried. Really. I did. Suddenly, who I was and who I was trying so desperately to hide from came to the surface, right there on the beach. In a split second, reality came at me with a vengeance. "Oh my God! I really *am* a Lesbian." Always have been. I grabbed my bag and I went to my room feeling euphoric, free, and so splendidly me.

I couldn't wait to get back home. I looked up and joined every gay event I could find. I was rapidly allowing my life to unfold. The light that shined on me when I burst open that closet door was so bright, so warm, so comforting. The tears that flowed from that feeling of freedom – I won't even try to describe it. I can't.

Fate has been good and I have met the most amazing woman ever. My boys love me and are not ashamed of me. I've made friends who have inspired me and who love me as much as I love them. I thank them all.

THE IGNORANT MRS. WATT

MRS. WATT
(Sits center stage wearing knee-hi stockings, slippers, a sweater, and a long skirt.)

I have lived next door to The Mendoza family for thirty years. Ever since my husband, rest his soul, and I were newlyweds. The Mendozas are, oh how can I say this, they are *(she cups her hand around her mouth and whispers)* Puerto Ricans.

Well, I didn't know. This is a nice neighborhood. Besides, by the time we found out they were living next door, it was too late. We had already bought the house. I must say though, they were the only neighbors who came over to welcome us to the neighborhood. They came over with their five children. Five children! Aha. They were very nice. They bought over some cold cuts, rolls, and Café Bustelo. You ever had that Cafe Bustelo? Good Lord. Kept my husband and me up all night. That's okay. We were newlyweds, so we didn't mind. We made good use of the time. Café Bustelo. Lord, now I know why they're such hyper people. Drinking that stuff all day and not getting any sleep, you would be too.

We lived for years next door to The Mendozas. Still do. *(Looks over and hollers)* "Good morning Mrs. Mendoza. My! That's a pretty red blouse you're wearing. Have a good day."

(She addresses the audience again.)

Lord, will you look at that blouse. It sure is red. Well, you know. Oh dear, where was I? I lost my train of thought. Oh yes. Their five children grew up to be real good kids. Not one of them ever went to jail. I know, right? Hard to believe.

The oldest daughter, though, she was quite the little rebel in her teenage years. One night she came in late and I could hear them reprimanding her. Then suddenly it got quiet. Later that evening I saw Mr. and Mrs. Mendoza drag out a rolled up carpet and put it in Mr. Mendoza's truck. I thought they murdered that poor child for sure. My husband, rest his soul, told me that I had an overactive imagination from watching too many detective movies. So I waited till it got real late and I went over to investigate. I was with the neighborhood watch, you know. I pulled the carpet out of the truck. Yes I did. It was an open pickup truck. I unrolled the carpet and…that's all it was. A rolled up carpet. No dead body. Well, I had to check. Neighborhood watch, remember? My big mistake was, when I turned to leave, I knocked over the recycling bin. The sound that those cans and bottles made crashing against the ground at that hour of the night. Good Lord! All the dogs in the neighborhood started barking. The Mendoza's porch light went on and I ran like hell. Mr. Mendoza yelled out, "Stop!" I didn't. A little while later, the police knocked at my door. They actually called the police! Can you imagine the audacity of these people? Cops asked if I heard or seen anything. I told them, "No, I was sleeping."

Now, their middle child is a, oh how can I put this? He is a (*looks around and whispers*) homosexual. Shhh. I felt sorry for that one.

I remember one Saturday afternoon, I was out here watering my roses when I saw him, the little homosexual, ride by on his bicycle. He must have been about twelve at the time. A few minutes later, he came running around the corner. Shirt torn, nose bloody. He was beaten up then chased by a group of boys who were making fun of him. Then I realized he was not on his bike. Those little sons-of-bitches took his bike and were chasing him…with his own bike. Calling him a sissy boy. It was terrible. They almost caught up to him and I yelled out, "Hey, you stop that! You leave him alone." Suddenly, that little (*whispers*) homosexual ran onto my porch and into my house. That poor little thing was as petrified as a fox being chased by a pack of dogs. Hysterical crying. Once I got him to calm down, I cleaned him up and gave him some ice cream then walked him home. His mother was so appreciative. She cried. They are very emotional people, you know. His siblings wanted to go after the kids who beat him up, but Mrs. Mendoza wouldn't allow it. I have to admit, when I got home, I cried. That poor child. After that I could not keep that boy out of my house. It's like I became his buddy. I didn't mind. He was such a good kid. I mean, it's not like he can take a pill to cure himself. Or can he? No. I don't think so…right?

Anyway, he's grown up now. Such a handsome young man. And smart. He was in his senior year in high school. I believe it was his senior year – yes his senior year – I was getting ready to go to a wedding. I had on a lovely, velvet, midnight blue, off the shoulder gown. It was a formal wedding. Ben, that's his name… (*whispers*) the little homosexual. Ben came over to bring me a clutch bag his mother lent me for the wedding. When he saw my hair down, he said, "Oh no, Mrs. Watt. You have to wear your hair up with a dress like that. He had me take out my bobby pins and my Aqua Net hairspray. Then he put my hair up in a lovely French twist, and I must say I believe I outshined the bride. Funny how he did not grow up to be a hairdresser like they all do. I know, right?

He went off to law school. He passed the bar on his first try and he became a criminal attorney. One Christmas when he came to visit his parents, he came over to see me like he always does. He brought a *friend* with him. His friend is (w*hispers*) black. Or as they say nowadays, African American. He introduced his *friend* to me as his partner. They're both lawyers so I assumed they had a law firm together. Well, I didn't know. All this new fancy talk.

My friend Louise, her daughter Mary is a *(looks around and whispers)* lesbian. Shhh! Don't say anything. Louise doesn't think anyone knows, but I always knew. When Mary was a child, I could clearly see it in her. She was all the little tomboy. None of those little brats teased her, I'll tell you that. She could beat up any boy in the neighborhood. Yep, I saw the writing on the wall with that one too. Anyway, when Mary introduced her *friend* to me as her domestic partner, I thought they owned a cleaning service business together.

Yvonne Hernàndez

All this fancy beat-around-the-bush talk. In my day, those people called each other what they were—lovers. I believe homosexuals should go back to using that word. Lovers. Lovers! Now I can respect that because it's calling it what it is. That's right. Stop confusing me! Today, they do not have to fear persecution, yet they hide the word with fancy nonsense. Partners and Domestic Partners, my ass.

He's a good kid, Ben. That's his name. Well, he's a man now and he always makes sure to come over to see me when he visits. When my husband, rest his soul, passed away... *(Mrs. Watt chokes up)* Ben and his lover took time off to come to the funeral. And not just the funeral. They stayed with me for a few days. They cooked for me and helped me keep my house clean and in order.

(Beat)

I finally saw Ben. I mean, I really saw him for the first time. There was nothing wrong with him like I always thought. His parents did nothing to cause him to be a... *(she holds her head up)* a proud gay man.

I'm going to my first gay wedding this weekend, you know. Mary the tomboy is going to marry her lover. Ben and his 'now' husband are also invited and they're coming

8

over early to help me dress and do my hair. I love that boy and he loves me and he is *my* friend.

IT'S A LESBIAN THING

We were together for a while and it was great. I kept waiting for the ground to open up under me. It was scary. It was all going too well. I was waiting for the real world to come crashing down on me. Her friends said they loved the way I looked at her. Was it the same way I caught her looking at me? She was so devoted to her mother. If you ever see anyone treat their mother badly, run the other way because that is the way they will treat you.

She was sweet, too. The things she would say. She'd say, "I love that you're my girlfriend and I want to be with you always." I love the way she caressed my hand as we walked. How I missed that. Simple little things. She made me laugh. I loved falling asleep on her shoulder. I was so comfortable there.

I would tell her how much I missed her and she would tell me. It's funny how we actually counted the hours until we would see each other again. The last minute was always the longest. Yet, when we were together it seemed as if our time together went by in a second.

Well, so much *did* happen. The real world *did* come crashing down on me. You see, she had this ex-girlfriend that she just couldn't break ties with. Ties that I didn't want to get tangled in. She said that *I* had to make sacrifices in love. I'm not good with sacrifices. I'm not Jesus. My sacrifices are not that great.

That's all in the past now. So, all I have left are memories and gratitude for having known her. And, of course, we have to do the Lesbian thing. We're still friends and I'm friends with her girlfriend which is an ex of my ex-girlfriend who is an ex to me who is an ex to her girlfriend. You got that? Never mind. It's a Lesbian thing.

WHERE IS MY LOVE
A two woman monologue

Two women enter wearing their comfy house clothes. Each sits at a separate table with a cup of coffee.

1

Where is my love? I'm still waiting to find her. I've been in fruitless relationships. Some have been very nice, but you see, my true love and I have not met yet. I'm sure she is out there somewhere. Probably wondering where I am because she too has been in nowhere relationships. Sometimes I think I'll see her across a crowded room. Like the song. Or maybe we'll meet in a very romantic way. Maybe while vacationing. Right there. Right in front of the Taj Mahal. *(Beat)* Listen to me. I need to wake up. I have another book to read anyway. Well, I can always start knitting again. I love to knit.

2
(Stands and walks center stage)
How will it happen? How will we meet? Will it be like one

of those wonderfully corny Hallmark movies where I venture into a small town and there she is? Riding on a beautiful black horse. She's wearing a flannel shirt and her hair is blowing in the wind. Or maybe she will venture into the city. She is lost and she will ask me which train will take her to The Met. Nice! She loves the opera as much as I do. Then Cupid will do what Cupid does best, and he sends an arrow through both our hearts, and violins will play. *(Beat)* Or maybe we'll never meet.

1

No. Don't think like that. (*Stands and walks center stage.*) I know. Maybe one day we'll both decide to put down that book.

2

We'll forget the crowded rooms.

1

We'll get introduced by friends we both happen to know.

2

We will talk endlessly for hours.

1

Of how we both love those corny Hallmark movies.

2

Of horseback riding.

1

Or of holding hands in front of The Taj Mahal.

BOTH

Then I could say I found my true love.

2

I could see it now. I could tell her. *(Looks at 1)* We could get tickets to the opera.

1

I could see it now. She'll tell me we could get tickets for the opera. *(Looks at 2)* Really? I'd love that. I love the opera. I like to knit. Do you knit?

2

No. But I could learn.

1

I can teach you.

2

I'd like that.

1

I make really funky sweaters. I can make one for you. I can see you in the perfect one.

2

I can't wait to wear it.

(*Both ladies look sad again*)

1
(*Sits*)

She will look lovely in that sweater.

2
(*Sits*)

She will be lovely. *(Beat)* It's silly, but that's how I imagine I will meet her... someday...

1

Me too.

(Lights out)

FLAWED LIKE ME

Online dating. Yes, it's so much safer than the bars. Right. I tried it. Online dating, that is. Well, and the bars. The people on these sites go on about their job and their materialistic possessions. One woman posted her three-story, five-bathroom house and that's wonderful for her. Now tell me about your flaws.

I posted that my flat is small and cozy. I had to fill in the fact that I have some college—fancy for *no, I did not graduate*—that I have a cat, and whether my body is full, average, or sporty. I had to fill in the fact that I don't smoke. I get a kick out of the ones who fill in, "Trying to quit." That means they smoke like a chimney. Please don't misunderstand. I am not knocking smokers. Those who smoke should just fill in that they do. This way they can meet another smoker who won't bore them with their nagging, anti-smoking, righteous indignation and they can smoke themselves into a heavenly cloud and live happily ever after.

I wanted to fill in that I enjoy the freedom of nude beaches. They said, "Oh no, you can't fill that in." Why? So she can find out later that I like nude beaches, gets turned off because that's not what interests her, and there goes all that time wasted. I want someone who reads in my bio "Nude beaches" and she says, "Yes, that's the woman for me." I want to fill in that I don't care if the toilet paper is under or over and that at times we may find a towel on the bathroom floor and we'll laugh because it's okay. I'll just pick up the darned towel and I know she will do the same for me. It's okay because we *were* happy when we shopped and bought that towel together.

Online dating has worked for many people and that's wonderful. I want to start an online service for people who are a bit eccentric. For people who don't care if the toilet paper is under or over and who don't have tan lines.

FAITH and CAMILLE

CAMILLE *sits in her living room. She picks up a magazine and covers herself with a blanket. There is a knock at the door.* CAMILLE *answers. Enter* FAITH.

FAITH

Hello, Camille. I'm sorry. I should have called. I didn't stop to think that maybe, well, maybe you would have company.

CAMILLE

Faith…It's okay. How are you? You look great.
        (CAMILLE *straightens her hair and clothes.)*
I must look a mess, ha?

FAITH

Not at all. You look beautiful.

CAMILLE

Come in. Wow. I'm just glad I'm home and I didn't miss you.

FAITH

I remember how you love to stay home on Sunday nights.
If you weren't home, I would have left.

CAMILLE

No! Don't ever do that. If I weren't home, all you would
have to do is call me and I would come straight home. Or
you could come in. Do you still have the keys?

FAITH

Yes, but I thought you would have changed the locks by
now.

CAMILLE

No.

FAITH

Can I sit down?

CAMILLE

Yes. I'm sorry, sure, come in, sit down.
(CAMILLE *rushes to remove the magazine
and blanket from the sofa. She hurriedly
throws them behind the sofa. Again, she
straightens her hair.*)
Are you thirsty? Hungry? Can I get you something?

19

FAITH

Do you still keep Scotch in the house?

CAMILLE

I always do. It's your favorite drink. Ah…I'll just…I'll go get it.

(CAMILLE *goes to the cabinet.*)

FAITH

Will you have a drink with me?

CAMILLE

Yes of course. No ice. Right?

FAITH

Right. Hey, you have new furniture.

(CAMILLE *hands faith the Scotch.*)

CAMILLE

Yes. All except for the bedroom. I couldn't let go of the…bedroom.

(FAITH *quickly drinks the Scotch.*)

CAMILLE

Faith, honey, are you alright?

FAITH

I'm fine, but I could sure use another drink. Have you ever had one of those, "I just feel like getting drunk days?"

CAMILLE

Who hasn't? *(Pours Faith another drink.)* Are you driving?

FAITH

Yes.

CAMILLE

Then you are going to stay here tonight.

FAITH

What?

CAMILLE

You will stay here tonight because you are not getting behind the wheel after downing Scotch. You can stay in the bedroom. I'll sleep here on the sofa.

FAITH

I wouldn't want to put you out.

CAMILLE

It's okay. You can put out...I mean, you won't put me out.
Deal?

FAITH

Deal. Camille, you're an angel.

CAMILLE

Yeah, I know.

FAITH

Why are you being so good to me? After the way I hurt
you.

CAMILLE

That was a two-way street. Let's don't talk about the past.
        (FAITH *takes a long sip of her drink.*)
Hey, you need to ease up on that. Have you had dinner
yet?

FAITH

No.

CAMILLE

Let's order dinner.

(*She tries to take the drink from Faith.*)

FAITH

(Holds on to her drink.)

Okay, but after I finish my drink…Hey, where's Ajax?

CAMILLE

I had to put her to sleep.

FAITH

No! What happened? Why didn't you call me? Let me know? I would have been here for her.

CAMILLE

Faith, it was such a rough time for me.

FAITH

It was for me too.

CAMILLE

Please understand. I couldn't think clearly. I didn't know what to do.

FAITH

I'm sorry. I know you didn't deliberately leave me out of it. It's not your nature. I understand. Poor Ajax. She was such a goofy cat. I remember when we found her. She was crying in the alley out by the deli. She was such a tiny little thing. All curled up and cold inside of an empty box of Ajax. She had a bloody paw too, didn't she?

CAMILLE

Yes she did.

FAITH

We put flyers up everywhere, but no one ever claimed her. She was so young. What happened to her?

CAMILLE

She developed a respiratory infection. She was in so much pain. I guess she wasn't so lucky.

FAITH

She was very lucky. She had you.

CAMILLE

She had you too.

FAITH

No, she didn't. I never even called to check on her. I'm such a terrible mother.

CAMILLE

Stop that talk! She loved you and she missed you. She always slept on…your side of the bed.

FAITH

Go ahead. Make me feel worse.

CAMILLE

I'm not trying to do that. I know we can't replace Ajax, but we can always get another… kitten. *(BEAT)* So, what have you been doing with yourself?

FAITH

I live in Brooklyn now. Red Hook. I have a cute little studio there. You should come see it. It's very quaint but…I really miss this place.

CAMILLE

And I...and this place misses you. Are you with…anyone?

FAITH

No. Why would I want to put myself through *that* nightmare again?

CAMILLE

Nightmare? I was not a nightmare to you!

FAITH

Pump your brakes there. I wasn't talking about you. I was with someone and she was the nightmare.

CAMILLE

You were with someone? Really? I tried that. I couldn't. I loved *you* too much.

FAITH

Loved?

CAMILLE

Love. Faith, I go through the motions every day. I go to work. I have my paintings. I'm still acting at the local theaters. I've even had a couple of lead roles.

FAITH

Camille, honey, that's wonderful!

CAMILLE

Yes the great white way hasn't discovered me yet.

FAITH

Their loss.

CAMILLE

Yeah, well, tell them that, will you please? ...You know I'm really surprised by your visit.

FAITH

(Stands and turns her back on CAMILLE, feeling the effect of the alcohol.)

I miss you. Oh hell, Camille. I still love you. I always have.

CAMILLE

(Laughs sarcastically. Also feeling the alcohol. She slams her cup down.)

I see.

(She stands and walks slowly over to Faith and looks her in the eye.)

Let me see if I'm understanding this correctly. You and your "fly by night" girlfriend don't work out, so you decided to come crawling back here!

FAITH

Now, you wait a minute! I'm not crawling anywhere. I came back here because…because…

CAMILLE

Because what, Faith? Because you still love me? Because you're so sorry, so remorseful about how you tore my heart out? Because you want me to forgive you? Because you want to start over again? Or could it be that…

FAITH

Yes! Yes! Yes to all of the above. I love you and I'm sorry! I'm sorry! I'M SORRY!
(Calms herself and sits.)
I do love you, Camille. I do. I do.

CAMILLE
(Sighs)
I know. I love you too.

FAITH
(Points in CAMILLE'S face.)
And don't you jump down my throat with your sanctimonious bullshit! You weren't so innocent yourself, you know?

CAMILLE

I know, I know. Faith, come on. Let's don't fight. Look,
I've got something to show you.

(CAMILLE *takes out a photo album and*
places it on FAITH'S *lap.* FAITH *slowly*
opens it.)

FAITH

Oh my god. All the places we've been to. Look! The Eiffel
Tower where you stood underneath and started singing
Broadway tunes in French. That was awful.

CAMILLE

Yes it was, but what a wonderful time we had.

FAITH

We had a wonderful time anywhere we went.

CAMILLE

True. Of all the places we went to, this one is my favorite.

FAITH

The fountain in Central Park? Of all of the places we've
been to, this is your favorite?

CAMILLE

Don't knock it. Just like we traveled to see other sights, others from all over the world travel to see that fountain. We spent a lot of time there. We enjoyed ice cream in the summer.

FAITH

Snuggled in the winter. Then we'd go home and have hot chocolate.

CAMILLE

With marshmallow. It will always be my favorite.

FAITH

Look, The Naumburg Bandshell where you recited Shakespeare's Sonnet 121. "Tis better to be vile than vile esteemed. When not to be receives reproach of being. And the just pleasure which is so deemed, not by our feeling but by others seeing. For why should others false adulterate eyes give salutation to my sportive blood? Or on my frailties, why are frailer spies which in their wills count bad what I think good. No, I am that I am and they that level at my abuses reckon up their own. I may be straight though they themselves be bevel. By their rank thoughts my deeds must not be shown, Unless this general evil they maintain, all men are bad and in their badness reign."

CAMILLE

You remember. Of course you do. You helped me learn it.

FAITH

You looked so confident on that stage. I was so proud of you.

(She picks up a Polaroid photograph.)

You still have this? This is the night we met at Ruby Fruit. I remember there was a cute little woman going around taking pictures and you called her over and she took our picture.

BOTH

Two dollars. Two dollars.

(They laugh.)

CAMILLE

I'll never forget that night.

BOTH

December 31, 1999

CAMILLE

You came in about fifteen minutes before the ball dropped.

FAITH

We met.

CAMILLE

We said good-bye to 1999.

FAITH

Together, we rang in a whole new decade.

CAMILLE

We hadn't even known each other's names yet.

FAITH

Yeah.

CAMILLE

We sang Auld Lang Syne. How corny.

FAITH

Very corny. Then we had this picture taken.
          (She puts the picture back into the album.)
Are you still writing?

CAMILLE

No. I really haven't been very motivated.

FAITH

Write about tonight.

CAMILLE

What do you mean?

FAITH

Write about tonight. About a couple who realized…they still love and want each other.

CAMILLE

Hopefully it will have a happy ending…Come on.
(She takes out menus and a game of Scrabble.)
Let's order take out and play a game of Scrabble.

FAITH

I'm not done looking at the pictures. Besides, don't you ever get tired of me kicking your ass at Scrabble?

CAMILLE

Don't flatter yourself. I've been going to game night at The Center and I've gotten pretty darn good at it.

FAITH

Hey, I'm serious. I think you should start writing again. I love your writing. I'm telling you, write a play about tonight.

CAMILLE

Seriously, Faith. Do you really believe anyone is going to dish out their hard earned cash to sit in a theatre to hear a story of two lesbians rekindling their relationship over Scotch, while they talk about their dead cat and a Polaroid picture taken some seventeen years ago?

(BEAT. *They look into the audience. The audience usually laugh at this. Then look at each other again and continue.)*

FAITH

Yes. Yes I believe they will. It's like that movie, "Write it and they will come."

CAMILLE

I believe that quote is, "Build it and they will come."

FAITH

Same concept. That's the point, Camille. They will come. I can see the audience now.

*(She stands center stage with her arms
spread out, looking into the audience as if
imagining it.)*

CAMILLE
(Takes Faith's hand.)
Come on dreamer. Help me pick out a menu.

*(They hold hands and just look at each
other for a beat. CAMILLE drops the
menus. They kiss.)*

LIGHTS OUT

SHE WAS STRAPPIN'

She embraced me. I felt something of a hard substance in her pants. Goodness! She was strappin.' She smiled a "cat that got the canary smile."

My reaction when I noticed that she was wearing this contraption was not of the glorious night that was to ensue. Nor was it, "Oh, this is exciting." No. My reaction was, "What if we get into a car wreck and you're unconscious, we're taken to a hospital, they take off your clothes and you're wearing this contraption? Wouldn't you be embarrassed?"

She said, "Why would I be embarrassed? I'm wearing clean underwear."

PRAY THE GAY AWAY
A comedy

Hello and good evening, ladies and gentlemen, and welcome to Pray the Gay Away. I see we have a few new recruits here tonight. Let us start by welcoming our new recruits. Let's give them a hand.

(*She claps*)

My name is Lez Bea Ann, President and founder of Pray the Gay Away. We are a much hated group because we spread the word that you too can be cured of this lifestyle called homosexuality. We know that homosexuality is a choice and we choose a normal life. We are not out of the closet. No. We are one better. We are out of the trap doors of our former lives. We are Gay no more. I want to introduce you to Lota. Lota Fish. Come on up Lota Fish.

(*Lota comes up and shakes hands with Lez.*)

Lota has been with us a year now and has earned her Pray the Gay Away pin. I don't know if you can see it, but this pin is shaped like a vagina and it has a red "X" over it. Isn't it cute?

(*Lez goes into a day-dream state.*)

It's...a little...vagina...so pretty...you can almost see and feel the clitoris.

LOTA
(Taps Lez on the shoulder.)

LEZ

Ha? What?

LOTA

You were going to pin me?

LEZ

What? Finger you?

LOTA

No. You were going to pin me?

LEZ

Pin you? Oh yes, pin you.

(She puts the pin on very close to Lota's breast, slowly. Lota fixes Lez's hair and they smile at each other.)

Let's give Lota a hand. (*She claps.*) Before we go any further. I want to read a little something that I wrote for Lota. As you all know, I have been her mentor through her ordeal to pray the gay away and I am so proud of her.

LOTA

Oh no, Lez. You didn't.

LEZ

I'm sorry, Lota. I know how much you hate surprises. This list is entitled, "The Things I Love About Her."

LOTA

Awe, I love you too, Lez.

LEZ

Okay. Here we go, The Things I Love About Her. (*Clears her throat.*) I love her wisdom. I love her kindness. Her thoughtful-ness. The compassion she shows towards others. She's sensitive. I love her willingness to learn.

(*She looks at Lota.*)

That one was our favorite, wasn't it honey?…ah, I mean Lota. I love her shy nature. Her bold nature. I love her…feet... (S*ighs*)

Oh, I'm sorry. Did I get off track? I'm sorry. You see, let me backtrack. I forgot to mention that Lota and I are writing a play of our former *wretched* lives and I believe some of the play must be getting mixed up with my list. Now let's see. Here we go… I love her smile. How she jumps up and down when she dances, just because.

(*Both women start to bounce around, dancing. Then realize what they're doing, stop, and straighten up.*)

I love her lips. (*Sighs*) Oh darn, did I do it again? I am so sorry. I'm getting the character that I'm to portray for our upcoming play about two women who find true happiness in their new, normal hetero lives. See, I'm getting it mixed up with my letter here. Let's see… I love how she loves her family.

She loves trucks, books, and jazz. Just like me! I love how she loves construction and building things. Ahh, she's so good with her hands.... Oh, we love to shop together. Like the other day when we were at her favorite sporting goods store and I helped her pick out a tight fitting jogging bra and it looked so darn good on her. Holy Moly, hot dang! Oh, back to the list. I don't know what's wrong with me today… I love how she loves her cat. She has this cute little peach fuzzy pussy that we pet every day and when she bends over to feed the little darling, you can see the elastic on her boxer shorts. Right back here.

(*She points to the back of her pants.*)

The boxers I bought to match her jogging bra. Sometimes, depending on the jeans she wears, I can see a little butt cleavage. So cute. Lota you are too much. I'm sorry. You'll have to excuse me. I'm nervous. You see, we're writing this play and it's all getting mixed up here…I told you that already, didn't I? Now, back to the list. Yes, but most of all I loved every minute that I helped and mentored her through her whole ordeal to pray the gay away.

(*She fans herself with her papers.*)

Now if you'll excuse us, Lota Fish and I have to go back to our room because…well, we have to finish writing this play.

(EXIT: Running off the stage holding hands)

I KNEW IT

You left work at 5:30? I called you at five. You weren't there. What's that? Really? Well, I went to the pool hall. I thought I'd join you. You weren't there. I waited…

Please stop. I've known for so long. I felt it, here.
(Puts her hand on her chest.)
It's strange. I appreciate your lying to me. It shows that even though the love is gone, you're trying to spare my feelings. But, don't you see how cruel that is? Just tell me. Spare me the pain. They shoot horses don't they? Animals are put to sleep to spare them the pain. So, just shoot me now. Be kind. End this pain.
(BEAT)
I knew it. You know, just go. Get out! But please…don't go.

Is this happening? Good god. We've lived in this house for fifteen years and those few bags are all you're taking with you? It's funny. Suddenly, I'm having such ridiculous thoughts run through my head. I look around and I remember when we first painted this room. We argued, "This color is too light," or "This color is too dark," but we eventually settled on the perfect color. Together in this house we decorated fifteen Christmas trees. We popped open fifteen bottles of champagne to celebrate the New Year. Fifteen chocolate Valentine hearts, Easter bunnies, Fourth of July barbeques, Halloween pumpkins, turkeys, and shamrocks. We gathered how many bags of leaves and shoveled how many pounds of snow right outside our front door? God! These thoughts are so stupid but how can I think intelligently through all of this…pain?

We never had children of our own, but together we watched the children in our families grow, marry, and have children of their own. On the day of my mother's death, I never would have made it without your strong shoulder, your tender hand. And your sister. Who I loved as my own. When that dreaded disease ate away at her beautiful mind, body, and soul, we were there for her. Holding her hand till the very end.

(She gets furious because her partner turns away.)
Don't you turn your back on me! You look at me!
(BEAT)
Together we did not think we could make it but, together…we did.

Now, could you put all of that into a bag and take it with you? You can't. I won't let you. Those memories are mine. Invested with my blood, my sweat, my tears, my joys, my sorrows, my happiness. I wish I could tell you to find someone else. I wish I could ask you not to rip my heart out and drag it through a thorn bush, but you see, I can't ask you to do something that you've always done.

ALMOST LIKE FRIENDS

(1972 Pennsylvania. An Amish girl sits alone. Enter,
ANGELA, *a hippie girl. She sits next to* BETH.
BETH *moves over.* ANGELA *moves closer.* BETH
looks annoyed.)

ANGELA

Hello. Nice day to catch some rays…I get it. Still don't
want to talk to the likes of me. I'm surprised you haven't
ran away like the other chicken shit did when I tried to talk
to her. I guess I shouldn't say "shit" and shit like that to
you…Look, I'm trying to be friendly here. I bet if God
came down here right now, you would be the one he
reprimands for being so rude which, I am sure, must be
frowned upon in the Bible.

BETH

Do not take the Lord's word or the good book in vain.

ANGELA

Hey, she speaks.

BETH

Only to defend thee.

(She points up)

ANGELA

(Looks up)

Thee? Who? I don't see anyone… *(Laughs)* Be cool, man. I'm just jiving you. I'm sorry. I shouldn't have said that. I have to admit though, I think it's far out the way you defend your thing.

BETH

My thing?

ANGELA

Yeah man. Your thing. When you believe in something, it's your thing? You dig?...Are you going to answer me? Come on. Stop being so uptight. Talk to me, man.

BETH

I do not want to be rude. I need to be alone. I have to think. Please. Besides, I do not understand your English. Far out? And dig what?

ANGELA

Man, aren't you hip to normal English? Never mind. Look, I offer you peace and love.

(She hands BETH *a daisy.* BETH *does not take it.)*
You want my arm to fall off? You get it? You want my arm to fall off? You know, from the movie, "Lady Sings the Blues?" Diana Ross and Billie D. Williams? Never mind. What was I thinking?

(BETH *starts to cry.)*

ANGELA

I'm sorry. I know the movie was sad, but come on.

BETH

I am not crying over a silly movie... Not that it's any of your concern, but I am to be married in one month.

ANGELA

Bummer man... I'd be crying too.

BETH

Why do you call me "man?"

ANGELA

It's just a figure of speech. A slang.

BETH

I do not understand. Please leave me alone. You are confusing me.

ANGELA

Man, don't blame me for the whirlwind of confusion in your head. It was there long before I came along. What's happening? You should be happy. Don't you want to marry this guy?

BETH

This guy has a name. His name is Jacob.

ANGELA

I didn't know his name was Jacob so I called him "this guy." Man, you are one uptight chick.

BETH

Uptight?

ANGELA

Never mind. Now you are confusing me.

BETH
(Mimics Angela.)
Don't blame me for the confusion in your head. It was there long before I came along.

ANGELA
You didn't come along. You were here already. I came along, remember?

(The girls laugh.)

BETH
Alright…Is your offer for peace still open?

ANGELA
Yes it is.
(She hands BETH *a daisy.)*

BETH
These are lovely. Where did you pick these?

ANGELA
Just over there.

BETH
(Laughs)
That is my father's land. We just made peace with my
father's daisy.

ANGELA
Oops! Well, it's the thought that counts. I can't believe I
quoted that corny cliché.

BETH
It's a lovely thought. Thank you.

ANGELA
So, tell me about this future husband of yours.

BETH
I cannot speak of this to you.

ANGELA
Sure you can. I just gave you a daisy. Besides, you bought
it up.
(She closes her eyes and raises her palms towards the sky.)
Wait a minute. My vibes tell me you need someone to talk
to because... *(Again looks at* BETH.) You don't want to
marry this Jacob. Rap to me, baby. Don't fight the energy.
Let it flow.

(*Hands* BETH *another daisy.*)

BETH

Jacob and I have known each other since we were children and I do love him, but not that way.

ANGELA

That's it. Keep going. Let it go. Keep rapping to me, baby.

BETH

I believe a woman should love a man. But, it is best for me to marry. When one marries, the man can be the head of the woman as Christ is the head of the man.

ANGELA

You're jiving me, right?

BETH

Excuse me?

ANGELA

Are you serious?

BETH

Why would I not be serious? It is in the good book. If you would bother to look it up, you will see.

ANGELA

I will either marry or live with the man of my destiny only
when I fall in love and no one will be the head of me.
Anyway, I will not live with him until I am an old lady of
at least…30.

BETH

Or *live* with him? I do not wish to speak of this any longer.

ANGELA

Yes. Or live with.
(She stands, fist in the air.)
Equal rights. Justice for all, my sisters of suffrage who
paved our way out of the kitchen and into the voting
booths, for I am woman!

BETH

Alright! Will you please stop making such a spectacle of
yourself? My father will hear you. He will not appreciate
your being here.

ANGELA

Excuse me. Your property line is over there. This side of
the fence is public property, so your father can't say squat
to me.

BETH

What I mean is, he will not say a word to you. I would be reprimanded for being here. Please. I am woman too.
(*She timidly raises her fist.*)

ANGELA

Far out. You aren't such a square after all. So underneath all those threads lies the heart of a groovy chick.

BETH

Thank you. I think. What are you doing here so far from the tourists?

ANGELA

If you must change the subject, I just came from an Amish tour.
(*Both the girls laugh.*)
I had to get away from the fam for a bit. My little brother can be a real trip at times.

BETH

You have a strange tongue.

ANGELA

You should hear what you sound like from here. I'm surprised you're even rapping to me... Sorry. Talking to me. Tour guide said you all don't talk to us lowly outsiders.

BETH

That is obviously not true. We occasionally talk to you lowly outsiders.

ANGELA

Hey!

BETH

Tour guides. What do they know? I resent how they paint such an unjust picture of us. They know nothing of us, yet they are paid to tell the story of our lives. It is a disgrace.

ANGELA

He told us about a ritual you have called "A Sing." It's crazy, man.

BETH

It is not crazy.

ANGELA

I don't mean crazy like "crazy." I mean crazy like…craaazy. He said you girls start dating when you are about…ten.

BETH

That is a terrible lie!

ANGELA

I'm jiving you, man. Don't have a cow.

BETH

The Sing is a much needed event. I hope your tour guide explained that to you. Most likely he did not. The fortnightly evening of Sing is often held at the same house or barn as the Sunday morning service. It is the most common event for boy-girl association and are not be held until after all of the chores are done.

ANGELA

I would make sure not to make my bed on that day.

BETH

On the day of The Sing the males dress in their finest. Then he ensures his horse and buggy are clean.

ANGELA

Hot diggidy.

BETH

Why do you ridicule? It is so typical and very judgmental
of the English. Our women are not trapped or suppressed.
Now, if you will allow me to continue.

ANGELA

You changed the subject.

BETH

After you said "hot diggidy."

ANGELA

You don't know what "uptight" means but you know what
"hot diggidy" means.

BETH

Oh, never mind.

ANGELA

No. Tell me. I want to know…Really.

BETH

A young man must make sure his horse and buggy are clean and his sister must ride along.

ANGELA

What if he doesn't have a sister?

BETH

Our families are large enough to have sons and daughters.

ANGELA

No. Some families have all daughters. My neighbor has four daughters.

BETH

No sons? That is awful.

ANGELA

What! Why is that awful?

BETH

Without sons, the family name cannot be carried on.

ANGELA

The daughters are just as important. We are the ones who carry the sons in our bodies for nine months.

(Stands. Fist in the air.)

Power to my sisters who suffer the wonderful agony of giving birth to boys who carry on the family name.

BETH

Will you hush?

ANGELA

No! We must raise our voices and be heard.

BETH

Alright! Do you have to do it here?

ANGELA

Be cool, man.

BETH

You are the one who must be cool.

ANGELA
(Laughs)

That sounds funny when you say it….I never told you my name. I'm Angela.

BETH

Angela? Do you know the origin of your name is Latin and

its background is Christian? Derived from the Greek word, Angelos. Messenger of God.

ANGELA

That's cool. I didn't know that.

BETH

You were given a name and do not know its meaning? How typical. "Just give her a name because it sounds pretty."

ANGELA

Now who's being judgmental? Look, you told me my meaning. Now I know what it means.

BETH

My name is Beth. The name Beth roughly means "house." It is very common in the Bible. Beth is also the second letter in the Hebrew alphabet. This letter is also used in the meaning of "in" which makes my name the first word in the Bible. "In" the beginning.

ANGELA

Do you always go around defining people's names? You must be a real gas at a meet and greet.

BETH

Alright. Forget I said anything. Jesus!

ANGELA

Oh! You took the Lord's name in vain!

BETH

I did not... *You* are not easy to talk to and you keep
interrupting.

ANGELA

Peace, man...Hey, you want to see what I've got?

BETH

I am almost afraid to say yes.

ANGELA

(Looks around and pulls out a joint.)

Want to share?

BETH

I do not smoke.

ANGELA

This isn't a cigarette, man. Have you ever wanted to see
God?

BETH

Of course. I hope to see him on the day I leave this earth.

ANGELA

With this, you won't have to wait for that day to arrive.
You can see him now.

BETH

I do not smoke. Do you know tobacco is tainted and
causes diseases? It is most unnatural.

ANGELA

This is very natural. It comes straight from the earth to
your kitchen table. No middleman which means that God
put it there for us to enjoy.
(*She lights the joint, takes a drag, and hands it to* BETH.)

BETH

I must confess. I have heard of these funny little cigarettes.
I believe they are called "a joint."

ANGELA

Groovy, man! Wow! "In the beginning Beth," you hip, sly
fox you.

BETH

I have always been curious about them.

ANGELA

Here's your moment.

BETH

Well…as long as the Lord planted it.
(She takes a drag and starts to cough.)

ANGELA
(Pats her on the back.)
Take it easy. Go slow. It's always rough "in the
beginning," Beth. Ah, I kill me. With the next drag, try to
hold it in for a few seconds. It'll work better.

BETH

Work better?

ANGELA

Help you to see God sooner. You okay? Try it again. Take
your time…That's it.

BETH

You're right. It was better this time. Can I try it again?

ANGELA

Be my guest.

(*They sit quietly and smoke.*)

BETH

You are right.

ANGELA

About what?

BETH

I *am* one uptight chick. Hey, this shit made me see what "uptight" means. Cool.

ANGELA

Now you're getting it. So, tell me more about this Sing.

BETH

You want to sing?

ANGELA

You were telling me about the Sing. I want to know more.

BETH

More about what?

ANGELA

The Sing.

BETH

I can't sing. But my mother has a beautiful voice.

ANGELA

(Laughs because she sees Beth is high.)
We left off when you were telling me about the horse and buggy.

BETH

Oh, yes. At The Sing, the boys sit on one side of the table and the girls on the other. Jacob and I did not speak much, but enough to know that we should marry so we could have a boy to carry on his name. His son. My son! That I will carry in my body for nine months. Power to my sisters. I just thought of something. If I have a daughter, shouldn't she carry on my name? Yeah, it seems only fair.

ANGELA

You know, I never thought about that. You make an excellent point.

BETH

At The Sing, I sat next to…Abigail.

(Sighs. She unbuttons her blouse.)

You should have seen her. She was wearing a lovely new bonnet and she looked so precious in it. It cast a shadow over her beautiful eyes.

(Sighs)

ANGELA

Wait...a… minute. There goes my vibe again. Hold on. I feel…oh I dig. Wow! This is a crazy scene. You're not supposed to have those feelings.

BETH

What feelings?

ANGELA

You're a homosexual.

BETH

Shhh! Will you please! And how dare you call me such a terrible thing?

ANGELA

It is not a terrible thing. People have fought and died for it. I live in New York City. In The Village. And let me tell you, just three years ago the homosexual community had it up to here with being harassed and arrested for dancing at a bar with their lover and for cross dressing. It happened at a bar on Christopher Street. It also happened that they lost their queen, Miss Judy Garland, on that very same day. They were in the bar mourning her death and they were not in the mood for another raid. The cops went in like gangbusters beating up all your people and all hell broke out.

BETH

My people?

ANGELA

It turned into a three or four day retaliation. The Stonewall Riots. Have you heard of it?

BETH

If I tell you something, promise not to tell anyone?

ANGELA

Who am I going to tell?

BETH

On occasion when I go into town, I sneak and read the newspaper.

ANGELA

Without paying for it? That's stealing!

BETH

It is not. I put it back.

ANGELA

Take a few more drags and when you see God, you explain it him.

BETH

I will. But wait. Listen. I read about this Stonewall and you're going to think I'm silly, but…

ANGELA

But what?

BETH

I have wanted to visit this Stonewall. I think it is peculiar that there is a village in a city.

ANGELA

There was a parade on the one year anniversary of the riots. It was a small parade and it's gotten a little bigger every year, but mark my words, someday that parade will be an extravaganza. I imagine a year like (*current year*) with floats and balloons. Here's a thought. You'll probably be able to marry Abigail by then. Wow!

BETH

Marry Abigail? Don't be absurd. Maybe one day I will visit this village.

ANGELA

Why don't you? I can leave you my phone number. Call me. I could take you. You can visit. My parents are really cool people. Come on out and be free. Be with your people.

BETH

I told you they are not my people.

ANGELA

Abigail.

BETH
(Sighs)

Abigail.

ANGELA

Look at you. You swoon at the sound of her name. You sneak around to read about what's happening with the gays at Stonewall. They're your people all right.

BETH

You are wrong for sure. Romans 1:26 says, "God gave them over to shameful lives. Even there, women exchanged natural sexual relations to unnatural ones.

ANGELA

Sounds to me that it doesn't specify what is unnatural. It could mean heterosexual people who have sex without marriage. That's considered unnatural in the Bible. You're just assuming it's the girl-on-girl that is unnatural. It could have been made up by men who hate it! But love it.

BETH

Wow! What if I did misinterpret? That would be crazy. Tell me. Would you go to this Stonewall?

ANGELA

I might. I would go to support the gays, but don't misunderstand. I like dick.

BETH

That is wonderful. Do you think you will marry this
Richard?

ANGELA
(Laughs)

Beth. You are priceless.

BETH

Can I confide in you?

ANGELA

Sure. I think it's cool how you feel comfortable to rap with
me.

BETH

There is no one else here to talk to.

ANGELA

Gee thanks. Go ahead. Tell me.

BETH

I read a book titled, "Spring Fire" by Marijane Meaker.
She wrote it under the name of Vin Packer.

ANGELA

Vin Packer? Packer? Cool. You ever notice how some names match the person? Like Alexander Graham Bell invented the telephone. Packer.

(*Laughs)*

BETH

There you go again. Can you be serious for a minute? Don't ridicule.

ANGELA

Hey, be cool, man. I love my gay folks. Here, have another drag.

BETH

Anyway, this Marijane Meaker is a…a…

ANGELA

A lesbian?

BETH

Shhh! Will you please keep it down?
(*She feels the effect of the pot and unbuttons her blouse a little more.)*
You know what? That's exactly what she is…a…a…

ANGELA

A lesbian!

BETH

Yeah! She is woman too!

ANGELA

A lesbian woman!

BETH

Who is?

ANGELA

Marijane Meaker. The author you're talking about.

BETH

Right. The book is called "Pulp Fiction." It was published in 1950 and it sold over 1.5 million copies. I thought, 1.5 million copies? For sure there must be others who feel like…

ANGELA

Like you?

BETH

(Stands. Holds her head and looks confused. Looks like she wants to cry.)

No! Do not be ridiculous. This does not happen to my people.

ANGELA

Looks to me like it does. Hey, it's okay, man. Homosexuality does not discriminate. It's who you were born to be.

BETH

Do not say that. I was not born to be like that. God does not make mistakes.

ANGELA

I have to agree with you there. I don't think you're a mistake…Come on. Sit down and tell me. When did you read this book and where on earth did you find a book like that around here?

BETH

(Wipes her nose with her apron.)

I read it when I had my Rumspring.

ANGELA

A what?

BETH

Your tour guide did not tell you about Rumspring?

ANGELA

No.

BETH

Our young people are allowed to go outside of our land to explore the world. If we choose to stay, we do not have to return.

ANGELA

You came back?

BETH

I am here. If I stayed, I would be shunned. I would miss my family terribly and… I could not leave Abigail. She will have her turn at Rumspring next month.

ANGELA

Next month? Aren't you going to marry this Jacob next month?

BETH

Yes. Angela, I do not know what to do.

ANGELA

Does she feel the same way about you?

BETH

Yes.

ANGELA

Leave. When she goes, go with her. Look, the way I see it, you can either spend the rest of your life with someone you love or with someone you don't. Let's say you and Abigail don't work out. Who you are will always be within you. Eventually you would fall in love with someone else in a cute little bonnet. Get hip with it, man. This is something you can't run from.

(*A man's voice calls out,* "BETH!")

BETH

(*Jumps up and buttons her blouse.*)

That is my father. I must go.

ANGELA

Wait. I'm leaving tomorrow. Family vacation is over. I won't see you anymore.

(They look at each other for a beat.
ANGELA *fumbles in her bag for a pen and*
paper.)
Here is my phone number. When you go to New York…

BETH

If I go to New York.

ANGELA

When you go to New York. Call me. You can stay with us.
My parents are really cool people. Please call. We've
shared quite a bit. I guess I can say that…we're almost like
friends.

BETH

I would dare to leave out the word "almost."
(A man's voice calls out again. "BETH!")
I must go.

ANGELA

Beth.

BETH

Yes?

ANGELA
(Raises her fist)

I am woman.

BETH

I am woman…Angela…when you see your Richard, give him a great big kiss from me.

ANGELA

When you see Abigail, give her a great big kiss from me.

BETH
(With a coy smile)

I certainly will.

(BETH *exits)*

(ANGELA *picks up her bag and the flowers. She smiles.
Exit* ANGELA)

THE RAIN

The rain can be such an inconvenience. Just when you want to wear that new pair of shoes, there's the rain. After making love, it's so darn beautiful, isn't it? Songs have been written about it. "I want to go outside in the rain." "Walking in the rain with the one I love feels so fine."

I looked out of the window and I pressed my face against the cool glass. I watched the rain roll down, glistening from the morning sunlight. Nature's own work of art and it doesn't even need a paint brush. Amazing.

I turned to see her lying there. So still. Peaceful sleep. I kneeled beside her. I looked into her sleeping face. I could almost count her eyelashes. The sound of her breathing in unison with the rain was rhythmic. There was a damp chill in the air and I covered her body with the blanket. What a damn shame. It was like putting a cover over a beautiful sculpture. I wanted to wake her, but no, I let her sleep.

I closed my eyes and I made love to her in my mind. Like

a child playing make believe. Believing that all in my imagination was real. I could still feel her inside of me. Smooth, penetrating, sultry. She sighed a cute little sigh. She rolled over and got into that fetal position. Her cute, curvy bottom was just too inviting and I could no longer control myself. I crawled in under that blanket and I could feel her warm insides. So smooth. I could feel her open up like a freshly watered rosebud.

The room was quiet except for the sound of the rain and her insides being manipulated by my hand. Her eyes were closed, but her flirty smile – I knew she was awake. She moved her body with me. I could hear the rain and her moans and…I want to go outside in the rain.

THEY CALLED HIM "FAGGOT"

He was a privileged child. Born with a silver spoon in his mouth. How could this happen in his family? After all, tragedies like this do not happen to people of their caliber. Do they?

As a child, he secretly purchased false fingernails that he painted bright red. He pranced with a graceful sway. His pronunciation emphasized his S's and C's. Because of this, they called him faggot.

His heart skipped a beat as he admired his mother's closet which was laden with the most beautiful dresses made of the finest cotton and silk. He secretly tried them on. He loved how the fabric spun as he twirled, admiring his reflection in the mirror. He tripped in his mother's high-heeled shoes, yet with a graceful determination he would stuff the tips with toilet paper then proceeded to dance to the tune of Donna Summer's "MacArthur Park."

His father's cigar-aficionado companions, while visiting

one evening to enjoy a smoke and a port, witnessed this horrific child. Flabbergasted and under their breath, they called him faggot.

The help used the kitchen as the quarters where they mimicked and ridiculed him. They could not figure out this queer boy. They pitied his poor, unfortunate parents and could only imagine their disappointment and confusion as to why God had chosen to punish them with such a boy. The oldest cook nurtured and loved him unconditionally since infancy; she was the only one who did not chastise the child. As for the others, they laughed at him and under their breath they called him faggot.

That red dress in the window. Oh, that red dress in the window. He ventured into the boutique to try it on. The sales woman spewed at him and told him the dressing room was for ladies only. He felt this was a strange thing to hear. Before he knew it, the words projected from within his core and he shouted, "I am a lady!" The owner of the boutique stepped out of her office to attend to this commotion. She glanced at the sales woman and put her off, for now. Madam Store Owner proceeded to allow the boy to go into the dressing room to try on the red dress and when he emerged from that room, Madam Store Owner and the sales woman were awestruck at how magnificent that red dress cascaded over his beautiful figure and Madam Store Owner did not hesitate to tell him. The sale was made. The sales woman was fired. Madam was furious at how her employee was willing to allow a two hundred and fifty dollar sale just walk out of her boutique. As the sales woman stormed out of the store, she turned and with a scornful eye, she called him faggot.

Despite it all, he excelled and enjoyed his high school years. He was fabulous. The sounds of all the cruel and contemptible words did not shake him. He loved his friends, who were all girls, and they loved him. He loved shopping with them. Loved the pajama parties where he was able to help the girls with their hair, clothes and make-up. What he was best at were his studies. His girlfriends always received the highest grades when he helped them study. An intelligent young man with a bright future.

His body was found just one week before his high school graduation. A blunt force trauma to the head. Spray painted on his naked body was that word. That word. Up until the very last moment of his life, they called him…faggot.

NOT AS IT SEEMS

A two woman/man monologue

ACTOR 1

He comes home to the comforting arms of his lover to break the devastating news he just received from his doctor.

ACTOR 2

By the look on his face, his lover knows.

ACTOR 1

The news is not good.

ACTOR 2

The results came back positive.

ACTOR 1

"Are you sure?" his lover cried. "We'll get another opinion."

ACTOR 2

He said, "This is our third. It's time we face reality."

ACTOR 1

They now know it's too far gone…

ACTOR 2

…and that it's just a matter of time.

ACTOR 1

They held each other tight.

ACTOR 2

He has just been told by his cardiologist that he tested positive for viral cardiomyopathy.

ACTOR 1

A fatal heart disease. I'm sure you've seen the movie, "Beaches"?

ACTOR 2

I bet you thought we were talking about...

BOTH

Aids.

ACTOR 1

Well brace yourselves and don't fall off your seats.

ACTOR 2

Gay men do not suffer from just one disease.

BOTH

We are not *that* privileged.

ACTOR 1

We also get diabetes…

ACTOR 2

High blood pressure…

ACTOR 1

Cancer…

BOTH

You name it.

ACTOR 2

Try to imagine this.

ACTOR 1

Imagine if you could go through your whole life…

ACTOR 2

…not having to worry about any disease but one.

ACTOR 1

Honey…

BOTH

No one is that lucky.

TEQUILA ANGEL

I once had an amazing, committed relationship. The sad thing is that, at the time, I didn't know it. I remember when she wanted to go to Cancun Mexico because of an ad she saw in a travel magazine. I was hesitant. We owned a business together and I was nervous about leaving it in the hands of our manager. Eventually, she convinced me to go and I am so glad she did. Our manager ran the business competently and we had a wonderful time.

The day we arrived in Mexico was beautiful. The hotel was lovely. Our room had a breathtaking view of the ocean which was as blue as topaz. We spent a day snorkeling. The coral was such a vivid orange. Life under the ocean is amazing. We spent another day at the ruins. It was so spiritual. It was like stepping back in time. We spent the warm evenings walking on the beach and just being bummed out lazy.

One night, we decided to stay in and have a romantic Cancun evening in our room with the air conditioning off and with the sliding doors and windows open to let the warm breeze massage our bodies. We drank tequila. Let me tell you, the tequila in Mexico is slamming. After two shots, I went into a hallucinogenic state. I felt as if my feet were not touching the floor. I was floating. Suddenly, I wanted to go swimming. It was late. I didn't go into the ocean, yet. I decided to go to the pool. I put on my bathing suit. Then I started to feel as if the bathing suit was an extra layer of skin and that there was a layer of slime on my body so I stripped off my suit, stumbled to the pool, and I jumped in butt ass naked because I had to wash this imaginary slime off of my body. It was a hot night and the water felt so cool. I looked up and saw my girlfriend standing at the edge of the pool watching me. She had an adoring smile and I could see love on her face. Yes, you really can see love.

She went inside to get the underwater camera. She joined me in the pool and proceeded to take pictures of me naked. She said I looked like a mermaid. Suddenly, I felt like a mermaid. I did not feel my legs. They felt strange as if they were turning into something else and I thought, *"Oh my god. I'm turning into a mermaid. I better get out of this pool quick because I am sure a mermaid cannot survive in chlorine."* So I took my naked ass out of the pool and ran toward the beach so that I could go into the ocean where mermaids belong. My girlfriend ran after me, trying to stop me from going into the ocean. She said that I told her that I had to swim out as far as I can so that I could join the other mermaids. I was not in a sane state of mind. I was tripping on tequila.

She finally convinced me to get out of the water. We lay on the sand with no blanket. We had sand in every nook and cranny. Then I looked up…and there she was. I saw an angel in a palm tree. The leaves were not leaves. They were her wings soaring in the breeze. She had a glowing face and she smiled at me. I said, "Oh my God! Look! There is an angel in the tree." I fell to my knees and I cried. Then I tried to climb the tree so that I could soar to the heavens with my angel. My girlfriend, again, grabbed me, this time to stop me from climbing the tree. I was so overwhelmed with this miracle, this angel that appeared before me. Is this La Virgin de Guadalupe? She did appear in Mexico many decades ago. Has she returned? Is there a message she wants to spread and she wants to use me to do it? I was so honored. The combination of the tequila and being overwhelmed by this angel made me pass out right there on the beach.

I woke up feeling euphoric and there was my girlfriend sitting at the edge of the bed with a cup of coffee. I apologized and told her how awful it must have been for her when I passed out. She laughed and said that I did not pass out. I guess I blacked out because she went on about the amazing sex we had and I don't remember a darn thing. Damnit! I believe there is a secret formula in the tequila that the locals sell to us tourists just so they could laugh at us.

I got out of bed and looked out at the palm tree where I had seen my angel the night before. I asked my girlfriend to walk out there with me because I had to see, this time with a sober head, if I saw what I thought I saw. We walked over to the tree. I looked up and...that's all it was. A plain old tree. The palm leaves were just that. Palm leaves. They looked nothing like angel wings. Now that was some far out tequila. That evening I drank water. I was tempted to drink the tequila again because, truly and in my heart, I wanted to see my angel again. Then I realized that I was just hallucinating the night before. Tripping on tequila. I really didn't see an angel but...till this day....I truly wonder.

YOU'RE MY SISTER?

BILLIE, *African American*
SARA, *White*

BILLIE *and* SARA *are lovers. Billie has been promoted to vice president of the company where she is employed. Sara has taken the day off to make everything perfect. She prepared a dinner to celebrate with Billie's boss and his wife who are coming over for dinner. Everything looks elegant – cream colored linen on the table, china and crystal. There is only one problem. Billie is very much in the closet at her job, something Sara has learned to live with. Until tonight.*

SCENE ONE

(Enter, BILLIE)

SARA

Hi sweetheart!

(She gives Billie a long, hard hug.)
How is my beautiful, smart, and talented Vice President?
Honey, I am so proud of you. My heart could burst.

BILLIE

Thank you, baby. It's like a dream. I could hardly believe
it myself.

SARA

Well, I can believe it because you are brilliant.

BILLIE

Look at all this! Everything looks so beautiful. Did I tell
you today how wonderful you are?

SARA

Yes, but you can tell me again.

BILLIE

You are wonderful.

SARA

Why, thank you, love. Oh, I almost forgot. I have to steam
the vegetables. What time will they be here?

BILLIE

(Hesitates)

Ah…they will be here at…7:30. You know, sweetheart. I keep my personal life to myself at work. I don't run around advertising that I am a…

SARA

A lesbian? It's okay. You can say it. It's not going to bite you. Come on, say it with me. A les…bi…an.

BILLIE

A lesbian. Alright. I am not one of those lesbians that goes around, fist in the air, "Hey everybody. Look at me. I am gay. Hear me roar."

SARA

I understand that, but what does that that have to do with you letting the people at work know that you are in a loving relationship *with* a woman? I'm not asking you to wave flags, and in case you haven't been watching the news, we can marry now. Your company will soon have benefits for same sex couples. They can't discriminate against you, so what are you afraid of?

BILLIE

Please, Sara. Let's not do this tonight.

SARA

Sara? Oh, I know where this is going when you call me Sara. Billie, they are going to be here soon. What should I do? Hide in the closet? Do I tell them I'm a neighbor who dropped by and I thought it would be fun to bring a couple of my pictures and put them in your living room?

BILLIE

There is no need to get upset.

SARA

No need to get upset! No need to get upset? So, what did you tell them?

BILLIE

I told them that…you're…my sister.

SARA

You told them I'm your sister?

BILLIE

Aha.

SARA

Honey, listen to me for a second here. You told them I'm

your sister. Don't you think there is a…*slight*…problem with that?

BILLIE

We have been together for eight years, Sara. We are very close. Like sisters. Get it? We do share everything.

SARA

No, Billie! I don't get it. We are not like sisters. But you're right about one thing. We do share *everything*… You have got to be kidding me. Oh, hell no!

BILLIE

Honey, please don't make too much of this. This is my job.

SARA

And this is my life. Also, what do you mean by, "making too much of this?" You make this sound like we're deciding something trivial here. You know what? The hell with this. If you want to live your life trapped in a closet, then you go right ahead, but you are not trapping me in there with you. Not anymore. Billie, honey, don't you see how much this is hurting me? How it's hurting us? You're ashamed of our relationship. Of me.

BILLIE

Don't you ever say that to me again! I could never be
ashamed of us or you.

SARA

No. Well how stupid of me for thinking such a thing.

BILLIE

Honey, you're just upset right now and…

SARA

You're damn right I'm upset. Upset and humiliated that
I've allowed you to treat me like this. No, this has gone on
for too long, but…no more, Billie. No more!

BILLIE

This day is so not turning out the way I expected. This is
supposed to be a happy occasion.

SARA

Well, excuse me for taking time off so that I could ruin
your day.

BILLIE

There is no need to be facetious.

SARA

(Takes a deep breath to control herself)

How dare you.

BILLIE

I'm sorry. I didn't mean it. I appreciate everything you've done. It all looks so beautiful.

SARA

Thank you very much, but you could have hired anyone to do this. The only difference is that they *would not* have done it with love and you wouldn't have to be ashamed of them.

BILLIE

Will you please stop saying that?

SARA

This promotion is such a huge milestone in your life. Something you have worked so hard for and I have been there every step of the way, as you have been for me, and I have to share it with you as a lie? As if I were some nothing. No, let me correct that. I am *not* a nothing. I'm your…sister!

(She calms down again. Billie tries to hug her. Sara walks away.)

I'll tell you what. I'll go along with this façade because I love you. I'll do this because I always felt, "If this is the only way she will have me, then this is the way I'll have to be." I'll do this because this is your day. Not our day as I so foolishly allowed myself to believe. Not anymore. I deserve better and I am out of here.

BILLIE

You don't mean what you're saying. Honey, I love you and you know it. You just can't leave like this.

SARA

Leave like this? You mean with what little dignity and self-respect I have left?

BILLIE

Look, sweetheart. Let's calm down here, okay? Look, let's wait for my boss and his wife to get here and after they're all settled, I will tell them everything. I will explain it all.

SARA

I cannot believe your audacity! I don't need you to explain me to anybody.

BILLIE

No. You're twisting my words.

SARA

Oh no. That is not allowed. You are not going to tell me that I am twisting anything. Not anymore…I'll tell you what, Billie. I love you and want to be with you more than anything. Now you have to do just one thing for me. If not, I'm out because I can't do this anymore.

BILLIE

Anything you want.

SARA

Tonight, you do the right thing by us. Prove to me that you truly love *us* and what *we* have. It's all up to you now, Billie. The ball is in your court.

(Exit SARA with BILLIE following behind trying to talk to her.)

SCENE TWO

(Enter MR. *and* MRS. SMITH)

MR. SMITH

Now, Eleanor, don't go having a few drinks and shooting off at the mouth. Billie's personal life is none of our business. She is competent and highly qualified which is why she was chosen by the Board for this position and that is that.

MRS. SMITH

For heaven's sake, George. I don't know what all the secrecy is about. Doesn't she know that everyone knows? You know the big talk around the water cooler is, "Why doesn't she come in already?"

MR. SMITH

That's "come out," dear.

MRS. SMITH

What's that, George?

MR. SMITH

I believe the phrase is, "come out," dear. Not "come in."

MRS. SMITH

Whatever it is, George, I'm trying to make a point here.
You know Gladys? In accounting? Gladys just got
engaged to her partner and now with this gay marriage
thingy, they're going to get married. George, we're having
a meeting about same sex benefits on Monday and Billie
will be at the meeting. Honestly, and what is all this talk
about her sister being here tonight? I know Billie has two
brothers. I never heard her mention a sister until today.
You know, George, Gladys says that she knows Billie is…
well, you know, that way because her gay radar is never
wrong.

MR. SMITH

That's "gaydar," dear.

MRS. SMITH

What's that, George?

MR. SMITH

Gaydar, dear. I believe the word is "gaydar." Not gay
radar.

MRS. SMITH

George, there you go again. You are missing the point.

MR. SMITH

Well, whatever it is, dear. It's none of our business if
Billie doesn't want to come out. You know, not all gays
want to wave and holler, "Hey look at me with my
rainbow flag and underwear. I am super gay. Hear me
roar!"

MRS. SMITH

Well, they're all doing it now, George. They are all flying
out of the closet.

MR. SMITH

That's "coming out of the closet," dear.

MRS. SMITH

You're doing it again, George. And how do you know so
much about their lingo?

MR. SMITH

I happen to live in the twenty-first century, dear. Everyone
knows the lingo except for you. As far as everyone coming
out, that's not true. Not for Billie, anyway, and I think that
should be respected. Now let's not talk about this
anymore. That's it! It! It!

(MR. and MRS. SMITH *knock at the door. SARA and BILLIE answer.*)

MR. SMITH

Billie. Thank you so much for inviting us. You have a lovely home. This is my wife Eleanor.

MRS. SMITH

We've met, George. At the Christmas party. Billie, it's so good to see you again and congratulations.

BILLIE

It's nice to see you again, Mrs. Smith.

SARA

Please, let me have your coats.
(Beat as MR. and MRS. Smith *look at* SARA)
Billie, where are your manners? You'll have to excuse Billie for not introducing us. She's excited, you know.
(SARA is a little flip and with a fake smile.)
Hello, I'm Sara. I'm Billie's sister.
(Shakes hands)

MRS. SMITH

Aha? Billie, you never told us you had a sister. Did she ever tell you she had a sister, George? Oh never mind.

MR. SMITH

I don't recall, but it doesn't really matter now, does it?

MRS. SMITH

I said never mind. This is lovely. Isn't it lovely, George?

MR. SMITH

Yes, dear. Very lovely.

MRS. SMITH

Billie, I know we shouldn't talk business tonight. I just want to mention one thing.

MR. SMITH

Eleanor, I thought we said we weren't going to talk business tonight.

MRS. SMITH

Just one quick thing, George, then I'll put it to rest until Monday. You know, Billie, we are going to have a very important meeting on Monday morning on...*same sex benefits*. I'm sure you're familiar with the subject?
(BEAT)
It's a subject that is very important to some of our employees. Which reminds me. Did you know that Gladys

in accounting got engaged to a woman? We need to get started on this right away, Billie.

BILLIE

What? Gladys got engaged?

MRS. SMITH

Yes. When her girlfriend, or should I say, her fiancé, came in to pick her up, Gladys got on one knee right there at the desk where they met and she proposed. It was touching. You were already gone for the day, dear, so you wouldn't have known.
(MRS. SMITH *looks at* SARA)
You should have seen Gladys. She was simply glowing.

(SARA *looks hurt but holds her composure.*)

MRS. SMITH

Sara, dear…are you alright?

SARA

Never been better. It's just that (SARA *holds her head up*) as a lesbian myself, this touches my heart. Isn't that nice, Billie? One of your co-workers got engaged. I can only imagine how happy and proud she must be. Can't you imagine it, Billie?

(MRS. SMITH *pokes her husband with her elbow.*)

BILLIE

No. I know how happy and proud she must be.

SARA

Well, let's go into the parlor for a cocktail. What will you have, Mrs. Smith? Mr. Smith?

(They start to walk away. BILLIE *does not move.)*

BILLIE

Wait! Sara. Please tell me you're not serious about leaving.

MRS. SMITH

Sara, dear, are you leaving?

BOTH GIRLS

No!

MRS. SMITH

Then you are staying for dinner? Didn't she say she was staying for dinner, George?

MR. SMITH

I'm confused, but I'll have a beer. Imported, if you have it.

SARA

Yes we do.

MRS. SMITH

I'll have a double scotch on the rocks.

SARA

That's my drink too, but I'm not having a double.

MR. SMITH

My wife can drink any man under the table.

MRS. SMITH

Or any woman!

(They all laugh as they start to exit)

BILLIE

I said wait! Please!

(BILLIE *walks to* SARA *and takes her hands.)*

Mr. and Mrs. Smith, Sara and I are very close, but she is
not my sister. I'm sorry I lied. I've been lying about
everything. About our wonderful life together and because

of it, I am about to lose the only woman I have ever truly loved. Honey, I've never felt such fear until tonight when you said you were leaving. It cut right through me. Nothing means more to me than you, my love. Nothing. Sara is not my sister. She is my lover, my partner, my everything, and I am extremely proud of her. Baby, please tell me I haven't thrown it all away. You said you'd give me this last chance. The ball is in my court, you said. Please tell me it's not too late to ask you to marry me.

SARA
No, love, it's not too late. Of course I'll marry you. I love you so much.

MRS. SMITH
I knew it! I told you. Didn't I tell you, George?

MR. SMITH
You told me. You told me.

MRS. SMITH
Wait till I tell Gladys in accounting. Billie. You just proposed, but I don't see a ring. Gladys had a ring. Didn't she have a ring, George?

MR. SMITH

Yes she did, dear.

MRS. SMITH

You are going to give her a ring, aren't you, dear? Or is that something lesbians do? Sometimes there's a ring, sometimes no?

MR. SMITH

Eleanor!

MRS. SMITH

Well, I don't know, George. I'm just asking. I mean no offense. Jeez, everyone these days is so word-sensitive. Wait till I tell Gladys.

BILLIE

We're sorry. Honey, we're being rude to our guests, and to answer your question, yes. We will go ring shopping tomorrow. Okay, sweetheart?

SARA

Yes, of course.

MRS. SMITH

Billie, it's none of my business, but you should have come in a long time ago.

MR. SMITH

Come out, dear!

MRS. SMITH

Don't be ridiculous, George. We just got here.

MR. SMITH

Never mind, dear.

BILLIE

I understand what she means, Mr. Smith, and I must agree with her. This feels wonderful.

MRS. SMITH

So, Billie, a promotion and engaged on the same day. You are one lucky lady.

BILLIE

I sure am. Hey, what are we waiting for? Let's go have that drink.

(SARA *and* BILLIE *exit)*

MR. SMITH
(Takes his wife's arm)
Dear, wasn't Billie's sister going to join us?

MRS. SMITH

Oh, for heaven's sake, George. Weren't you listening? What planet are you on?

MR. SMITH

I was listening. It's just that…..
(They continue to argue as they exit)

THE BEST I COULD

A woman faces the audience and speaks to her daughter.
Woman has a Southern accent. Daughter (not seen)

Well, Emily honey, I did the best I could. You were only three months old when your daddy up and died on us. Ever since then it's been just the two of us and I did the best I could. I did have a couple of gentlemen callers. I could have given you another daddy – a good daddy. I'm so blessed to have had a good head on my shoulders about picking a good man. Your daddy was a good man. Everyone says the reason I am still alone is because I was always trying to find a carbon copy of your daddy. I guess they were right. We were very happy, Emily honey, but only for a short period of time. It's unfair how he just up and died on us. Well, I didn't know that was going to happen and I did the best I could.

I'm not an educated woman. My mama, your grand-mamma, never encouraged me to educate myself the way I encouraged you. She comes from a different time, your grandmamma. She comes from a time when she encouraged us girls to…to be wives and mothers. Now there is nothing wrong with that and don't you *ever* let anyone tell you different. You know someone once called me a single mother. *(Laughs)* I am not a single mother. I am a widow. There is a difference. I *did not* choose this and I did the best I could.

I miss your daddy. I know, I know you've heard this a hundred times and you'll probably hear it a hundred times more, but I miss him. Oh, I loved him so. I'll never forget the first time I laid eyes on your daddy. He was the handsomest man in the room. It was at the annual Christmas ball. Everyone was dressed real nice. We all dressed up back then. I had on a pretty white dress. All we young ladies had to wear white. What is it about the color white that everyone thinks is so damn holy? I didn't want to wear a white dress. I wanted to wear a red dress like Bette Davis did in "Jezebel." Instead I put on my white dress and went to the ball. I walked into the room and…there was your daddy. *(Sighs)* He was just the prettiest thing.

(Fixes her hair)

You should have seen me. I know I took his breath away. He walked over to me and asked your uncle to introduce us. He was a real gentleman, your daddy. Then we talked and danced the night away. It truly was love at first sight. He asked me to marry him the very next day. My daddy wanted to shoot his behind. So we courted for a while just to keep your granddaddy happy. Eventually we married. You know, Emily honey, no one can ever stand in the way of true love. Not even a big strong man like your granddaddy. Nothing could stop him from cursing us either. He cursed us by not giving us his blessing. Then your daddy just up and died on us when you were only three months old. *(Takes out a hanky.)* And I did the best I could.

You don't know how surprised I was when I heard through the grapevine that you were seen in broad daylight, walking out of *that*…homosexual bar. I thought, "How nice. She has homosexual friends." I didn't know that, well that you were that way. I have to say…that was a tough pill to swallow. I asked God, "Why me? First you took my husband so young and now this." I thought, *(looks up)* "The curse continues. Thank you daddy…"

Oh no. Don't say that. That's what I thought at the time. I'm sorry I never said it before, sugar, but I don't feel that way anymore. My heart swells at how proud of you I am. Now I look at you, my beautiful daughter, my baby girl with your fine education, your fine job, your fine clothes, and how happy you truly are and I could see…there is no curse here. I am truly blessed. Then I get really angry at myself when I think of how I grossly underestimated myself. Because the best I could is obviously better than I ever gave myself credit for.

REMINISCENT HAUNT

(Two women enter. It is dark, raining. They are wearing rain coats and carrying a flashlight.)

OLIVIA

I told you to stop for gas but, no. "We'll make it home," you said. Now look. Here we are stranded in this god-forsaken place.

CATHERINE

Okay! So I miscalculated. I'm sorry.

OLIVIA

Miscalculated? When you see that little needle get dangerously close to that "E," that means WE ARE RUNNING OUT OF GAS!

CATHERINE

There is no need to get touchy about it. We're here now.

OLIVIA

Well, thank you very much! Catherine, let's get out of
here. This place gives me the creeps. What if someone
lives here? This is breaking and entering.

CATHERINE

We did not break in. The door was open.

OLIVIA

So what? Lots of people leave their door open.

CATHERINE

So, we didn't break in. We just entered.

OLIVIA

Catherine, stop playing with words and stop treating me as
if I were some kind of an idiot. You know exactly what I
mean.

CATHERINE

Alright, I'm sorry. Olivia…look. Look, Olivia! This house
is obviously abandoned. Why don't we just stay here until
morning? You know, I think it's a blessing we ran out of
gas. The roads are flooding and we couldn't get through
anyway. We could have gotten stuck and who knows what
creep we could have ran into.

OLIVIA

Yeah, that creep probably lives here.

CATHERINE

Oh, stop it. Honey, we'll call for help in the morning.
Okay?

OLIVIA

I don't think there's electricity here.

CATHERINE

We can charge our phones from the car. Olivia, get a hold
of yourself. The damage has been done and we certainly
are not going out in the dark with this wicked storm.
Relax, honey. Let's go upstairs. *(Flirting)* There are
probably beds up there.

OLIVIA

You're sick if you think I'm going to do anything in this
creepy old house. Honey, let's stay in the car.

CATHERINE

Stay in the car! Are you serious? We'll be safe in here.

OLIVIA

But this place is so dusty.

CATHERINE

Dusty. Olivia, look at us. We are muddy and dirty. I doubt
if a little dust is going to hurt us. Come on. Let's go
upstairs and look for those beds.

(*Catherine takes Olivia by the hand, flirting.*)

Lights out. Stage hand sets up bedroom.

Lights up. Enter, CATHERINE/OLIVIA

OLIVIA

Wow, this is nice and it's so clean and warm up here.

CATHERINE

See, I told you.

OLIVIA

Ah, Catherine, honey. Look, there are lit candles.

CATHERINE

Yes. Isn't it romantic?

OLIVIA

Honey. Lit candles! They did not light themselves.
Someone else is here.

CATHERINE

Olivia…I think you may have a point. Look, stay calm and let's just get out of here. We'll stay in the car.

OLIVIA

Now, why didn't I think of that?

(They start to run out. VICTORIA appears, wearing, faded, 50's clothing.)

CATHERINE

Oh my god! What, who is that?

OLIVIA

I don't know, but she looks like a cross between Norma Desmond and Mrs. Danvers.

VICTORIA
(Stern and stoic)

Who are you and what are you doing in my house?

CATHERINE

We are so sorry. We ran out of gas. We're traveling alone; we're scared and hungry and wet. We ran out of gas and we stopped here for shelter. We meant no harm. We're not thieves. We're so sorry.

OLIVIA

I told her to stop for gas!

CATHERINE

Will you shut up about the gas?

OLIVIA

Don't tell me to shut up.
(*They start to argue.*)

VICTORIA

It's quite alright. You ladies may shelter here for the night.
Max!

(MAXIMILLIA *appears. Also in faded clothing.*)

MAXMILLIA

Yes, my sweet?

VICTORIA

Maximillia, darling, these ladies are destitute. We must
help them. It is alright if they stay the night?

MAXIMILLIA

But, of course, my love. Ladies, you are welcome to stay
here. There is fresh linen, towels, and toiletries in the

cupboard. Tea and cognac in the kitchen. Please, make yourselves at home.

CATHERINE

Thank you so much. We promise we will be out of here first thing in the morning.

MAXIMILLIA
(Puts her arm around VICTORIA's *waist.)*
Come, my love…let's go to bed.

(As they exit, CATHERINE *calls out…)*

CATHERINE

Excuse me. Before you go, can we use your phone? Mine is dead and..hello…excuse me?

(Exit VICTORIA/MAXIMILLIA)

OLIVIA

Okay, they were weird.

CATHERINE

Don't say that. They were very sweet. You know what? I'm going to take them up on their offer. I'm going to have that cognac. Are you coming?

(CATHERINE *starts to exit.*)

OLIVIA
(Following close behind.)
Alright! But, if I get up in the morning with my head chopped off, I'm not talking to you!

(Lights out. Stagehand change to bedroom scene.)

Enter CATHERINE/OLIVIA

CATHERINE
(Yawning and stretching)
I slept so well. *(Flirting)* Thanks to you. How'd you sleep?

OLIVIA
I slept amazingly well. *(Flirting)*

CATHERINE
I'm sure you did.

(Enter STAN, *annoyed)*

STAN
Excuse me. I hope I'm not interrupting anything here, but who are you and what are you doing on my property?

OLIVIA

Oh my god, it's the creep.

STAN

Excuse me?!

OLIVIA

Don't come any closer or we'll kick your ass.

STAN

What are you talking about? No one wants to hurt you. Is that your car out there?

OLIVIA

I told her to stop for gas.

CATHERINE

Olivia, please! Look, we're sorry. We were stranded last night and…you know what? Never mind. We're leaving.

STAN

Hold on a second. We had a bad storm last night. I'm just glad you ladies are safe. Look, I'm going into town. I'll take the gas tank from the garage and bring back some gas for you ladies. You know, you shouldn't just walk into someone's house like this. You scared the life out of me when I heard voices up here.

OLIVIA

And you shouldn't leave your doors unlocked for any weirdo to just come walking in.

STAN

Yes, I see that now.

OLIVIA

Wait. What does he mean by that?

CATHERINE

Olivia, he's trying to help us.

OLIVIA

Alright. I'm sorry Mr…

STAN

My name is Stan. You can call me Stan. I own this house. And you are?

CATHERINE

I'm Catherine and this is my fiancé Olivia.

STAN

Nice to meet you ladies. You must be hungry. I just put some bagels in the kitchen. Help yourselves.

OLIVIA

Did you bring coffee too?

CATHERINE

Olivia!

OLIVIA

Well he said he bought bagels so I just assumed he had coffee too.

STAN
(Laughs)
Yes, there is coffee too. Help yourselves.
 (STAN *starts to exit, but is stopped by* CATHERINE)

CATHERINE

Wait. You said you own this house?

STAN

I just recently bought this house. I obviously haven't moved in yet. I've got quite a bit of renovating to do.

Plumbing is up to par so you have water. I'll return shortly.

CATHERINE

Wait. The ladies that were here last night said they own it.

STAN

What ladies?

OLIVIA

One of them was named Max?

STAN

You saw them?

BOTH

Yes!

STAN

Victoria Winslow and Maximillia Stone were school teachers in this town in the mid-nineteenth century. When the townspeople began to suspect that they were lovers, they were nearly tarred and feathered. They were awaiting trial, accused of corrupting the minds of the minor children. If found guilty they would have been sent to separate asylums or jailed and never allowed to ever see each other again. That never came to be because they killed themselves in this very room. Lots of people have seen them, but they are harmless. It is said they were very happy here.

OLIVIA

Apparently they still are.

STAN

Here's a picture of them.

(OLIVIA *and* CATHERINEE *are startled.*)

STAN

Well, let me go into town and get that gas for you.

CATHERINE

Here, let me give you some money for it.

STAN

Let's take care of that when I get back. See you in a bit.
(Exit STAN)

CATHERINE

Wow... Well, let's have some of that coffee.

OLIVIA

You go ahead. I'll be down in a bit.

CATHERINE

I'm impressed. You're not afraid to be alone here?

OLIVIA

No. Not anymore. Go ahead. Don't worry about me. I'll be right down.
(CATHERINE *hugs* OLIVIA. *Exits* OLIVIA. *Picks up the picture.)*

(Re-enter MAXIMILLIA *and* VICTORIA)

OLIVIA

I wish you could see how far we've come.

MAXIMILLIA

My lovely, look. She is wearing a gold band. The other young woman is wearing the exact same kind.

VICTORIA

They are married? To each other?

OLIVIA

(Does not see them, but answers.)

Yes, we are. Thank you. We can marry now, you know. I wish you were here to see it.

MAXIMILLIA

We are. Thank you.

(Exit OLIVIA)

VICTORIA

Did you hear that, my sweet? Our kind can marry now. Oh, my darling I feel so free. So gay!

MAXIMILLIA

My darling, I never thought we'd live to see the day.

VICTORIA

We didn't.

(They laugh)

MAXIMILLIA

Darling, we've always known that someday we have to leave this house.

VICTORIA

No. Yes, we've discussed it, but this is our home. We planted our hopes and dreams here. Do you remember our garden? Laden with the most beautiful roses.

MAXIMILLIA

Yes, my love, but those roses exist no more. We must move on, my love. I believe these young women were sent to us last night, my sweet.

VICTORIA

We have been here, loved here for more than a century.

MAXIMILLIA

That is but a blink of an eye when you think of the eternity we will be together. Victoria, my darling, you know that some of our students have lived the most amazing lives. Amelia Constance Fleming became the first woman doctor in this town. I pride myself in knowing that we had a massive influence in that. Bartholomew Lawrence Foxworth became a very well-known scientist and so many other children we taught have achieved great accomplishments. When we leave this house we will see them again. Talk to them. Hear their stories. Oh, Victoria my love, let us go. It is time.

VICTORIA

Do you know what I believe, my darling?

MAXIMILLIA

What is that?

VICTORIA

I believe the young women who visited us last night will not let our memory fade. The gentleman who bought our house, he seems to have an admiration for us. I believe that they will become very good friends and we shall live through their determination. They will not let our story die in vain.

MAXIMILLIA

They will not, my love. They will not. We *will* see them again someday. Come. Take my hand. We have all of eternity. It is time to move on.

(They start to Exit)

VICTORIA

Wait!

(VICTORIA *walks about slowly. Looking at the house for the very last time.)*

VICTORIA

I am ready, my love. Let us go.

(Exit VICTORIA/MAXIMILLIA)

LIGHTS OUT

THANK GOD FOR THAT

If anyone ever says to you, "No one will ever love you the way I did," what they are insinuating is that you will never be loved again. That is just not true. No one will ever love me the way you did? Well, thank God for that. You mean to be loved by magnifying my faults? To be loved by making me feel ashamed of the things I did for you just to make you happy? To be loved by making me feel like the dirt beneath your shoes? To be loved by constantly reminding me how wonderful you are and how wonderful I am not?

Fortunately for me, I have found someone who thinks my faults are cute. Someone who thinks the things I do for her are special and they are appreciated. Someone who looks up to me and not down at me from an exaggerated plateau of self-righteousness. I am now loved by someone who thinks I am wonderful because she is so wonderful herself.

No one will ever love me the way you did? Well, thank God for that.

OUR FIRST DATE

I love a woman who can eat raw fish. Sushi, oysters, clams on a half shell. I love a woman who drinks Johnny Walker Black. Straight up or on the rocks. No seltzer, none of that.

I was set up on a blind date. I live in New Jersey; she lives in Queens. We agreed to meet in Brooklyn. I rode the train because I'm not familiar with the area. She picked me up at the Atlantic Avenue Station in her cute VW. She looked good too. A Lauren shirt. Her jewelry was simple elegance. Small earrings and plain Movado watch with no bling. She smelled nice too. Not like perfume or cologne, but fresh like soap, shampoo, and tic-tacs.

In the car, we discussed where we should go for dinner. She suggested sushi. I thought, "Nice, she eats fish."

When I didn't answer because I was staring at her, she said, "Do you eat sushi?"

I said, "Yes, do you?"

She said, "I sure do."

So off we went to eat sushi. The restaurant was a quaint little place with white linen on the tables. I was about to suggest Sake, but before I could say a word, she asked if I would like to order Sake. So bring on the Sake.

During dinner, there was no awkward first date feeling. We talked and laughed as if we were old friends. One of the conversations we had was which cocktail we enjoy. I told her I enjoy Bacardi Rum. She told me she loves Johnny Walker Black. I asked her if she mixes it with anything like seltzer water. She said no, that she drinks it straight up or on the rocks. Oh, I had to cross my legs because I had an enormous hard on. Yes, women get hard ons too. When that little clitoris gets pumped and excited, it gets as hard as a pebble.

I was thinking about asking her if she would like to go dancing, but before I could say a word, she asked if I would like to go dancing. Is she reading my mind? So off we go to find a dance hall. Turns out she was a terrific dancer too. We went to the bar. I ordered my drink and she ordered hers. There was something about the way she said,

"*Johnny Walker Black, straight up.*" I had to sit down and cross my legs again. She asked me if I was alright and I told her that I just had to pee. Yes, I said "pee" on our first date and she thought it was cute.

After an evening of sushi, Sake, great conversation, dancing, and Johnny, she offered to drive me home. Back to New Jersey, mind you. But, we wanted to spend a little more time together. The evening just flew. We cruised around until somehow we wound up in her driveway. Then she asked if I would like to come in for a drink. I said no. After all, I have to be a lady. Then she asked if she could kiss me and I said yes. She kissed me and I felt the world spin. Then, I don't know how it happened, but suddenly my breasts were exposed. I also happened to be wearing one of those bras that snap in the front and she popped that baby open like that. *(Snaps fingers.)* Her hands and her lips were so smooth. Then I told her, "I think I will come in for that drink."

And in the morning....she made me breakfast.

CHOSEN LIFE

(A woman walks onto the stage. She is wearing a hospital gown. There is something unstable about her.)

Chosen. I was simply chosen to live the life that put me exactly where I am at this very moment. In this cold room with a metal framed bed and bars for curtains. People always make cruel remarks about the cake baking moms of the 50's. Me, I so envied them. I wanted what they had. A beautiful family. I never asked for this. I was put here by a power much higher than myself and I've had to pay with the rest of my life.

I was bad before I was born. Did you know that? So I was punished by being born to people who did not love me. They hated me. They resented me. My mother couldn't even look at me. My father, on one of his inebriated nights, beat the hell out of her. He broke her collarbone then raped her, broken bone and all. My mother got pregnant with me that night. You see now? I was a curse when I was conceived. I know all of this because my mother reminded me all of her life.

My mother couldn't stand to look at me. I don't blame her at all. You see, I was this awful thing that happened to her and because of it, she could never kiss. I never once felt the warmth of her breast because she never hugged me. She never once told me she loved me. She didn't. I could still see the contempt in her eyes. I could still feel the hatred resonate from her soul. I made her the way she was because I was born bad.

I also did bad things that angered my father. He would try to sleep late on Saturday mornings, but I would wake him when I played with my doll. My Nancy Nurse doll. Well, I had to be punished because on top of being born bad, I was ungrateful. My father worked hard so we could have the nice things we had and I thanked him by not allowing him to sleep.

Doctors all my life have told me that what he did to me was not punishment. That punishment is one thing and cruelty is another. If you ask me, the doctors are the ones who belong in here. What do they know? They weren't there.

(She walks about for a few seconds, lost in thought.)

I was just a little thing, playing with my doll. I disturbed his sleep. He got up and wrapped my long, beautiful hair around his fist and dragged my little body for what seemed an eternity. I was six years old. Then he stripped me bare and poured water all over me. Then he beat me with that thick, leather belt. The one with the heavy studs on it. Do you know what the water was for? It was so the whips could hurt even more. Which is stupid. What did he think? That without the water it would have been painless? He gagged my mouth so the neighbors wouldn't hear my screams. He tied my hands behind my back and made me kneel on metal cheese graters and locked me in the closet for my punishment. Before he closed the door, he took a large kitchen knife from the dish rack and made me watch as he plunged the knife into my Nancy Nurse. He cut out her eyes and stabbed her over and over until there were only pieces of her left. Then he threw the pieces of Nancy into the closet with me. He said, "Maybe next time you'll think twice before you wake me up with your goddamn doll." Then he closed the door. *(Angry)* Santa Clause gave me that doll and he had no right to do that! I loved her and he had no right to do that!

I don't remember how long I was in there. I do know that when he finally opened the door to let me out, the light that came in through the window hurt my eyes and the metal graters were stuck to my knees because of the dried blood. He yanked them off of my knees like pulling off a Band-aid, quickly so it wouldn't hurt. I think that was considerate of him, don't you? Then he poured alcohol all over my body. I can still feel how it stung. (*She rubs her body as if reliving the pain.*)

Don't look at me like that! He had to do it! He did it because he didn't want the bleeding welts to get infected. He did it because, in his own way, he loved me. The love my parents had for me was different because I was chosen. Born to be bad. Don't you see?

(*She calms down and gets lost in a memory.*)

I was a teenager when I met Wanda. It was the first day of school. She held her books tightly against her breast. How I envied those books. It was a windy September morning and her beautiful, black, silky hair was waving in the breeze. She took my breath away. I could feel my heart skip a beat. She caught me staring at her and I didn't care. I'm glad she saw me. She smiled and came over to me. As she got closer, my knees weakened. She said, "Hi, I remember you. We were in the same fifth grade class together. You sat in the last seat in the last row."

I was suddenly embarrassed. I'm sure she remembered how I never paid attention and how I failed every test. Our teacher's name was Mr. Cullen. He always laughed at me when he handed back my test paper with the big red "F" on it. I was also very quiet in the class. I stared out of the window, dreaming of the cookie cutting moms on those TV shows. Mr. Cullen always humiliated me by asking me in front of the whole class, what I was daydreaming about now, and that there was something obviously wrong with me, and the entire class laughed. Except for that one cute little girl that sat in the second seat in the first row. The one with the beautiful, long, black hair. There was something about the way she looked at me. As if she felt bad for me.

Then one day came when I just couldn't take it anymore. Mr. Cullen handed me back another test paper with yet another big red "F" on it and as he started to walk away he said. "Yes, class, our star pupil did it again." He held up my test paper and they all laughed. Except for the girl in the second seat in the first row.

I felt anger boil up inside of me and as Mr. Cullen walked away, I yelled out, "Go to hell you jerk-off. I hope you die!"

He turned around and looked at me with the same contempt in my mother's eyes and he said, "What did you say, you little shit?" He grabbed me so hard by the shoulder, he tore my dress.

(With an eerie tone)

He dragged me to the closet where the kids hang their coats. It was the kind of closet with the sliding doors with hooks that were used to hang coats. He tried to force me in there. To close me in there. I couldn't let him do that. Suddenly I felt this power come over me that I had never felt before. I grabbed a pencil from one of the students' desks. He had just sharpened it at that pencil sharpener on the windowsill. I plunged it into Mr. Cullen's arm again and again. The final plunge broke the tip of the pencil in his hand as he tried to defend himself, but I kept stabbing him over and over. I couldn't stop. Something came over me – a hysteria – and I just couldn't stop. He tried to grab me, but couldn't.

(Angry)

I wouldn't let him. He ran out of the class and I felt big. Empowered as the entire class looked at me and they weren't laughing. They looked at me with fear and respect and I realized right there at that exact moment, not allowing anyone to turn me into a mealy mouse was a power I could possess if I really wanted it. And, by God, I wanted it.

I got a taste of power and it became a drug injected straight into my veins and I was addicted instantly. It became the oxygen I breathed and the food that nourished my soul. Suddenly, I didn't hate Mr. Cullen anymore. I felt sorry for him. I appreciated him for bringing out a power in me I never knew I had.....That was the first time I was sent away.

I had forgotten all about that. It all came back to me when Wanda mentioned the fifth grade. Why should I be embarrassed? I held my head up, proud, knowing she must have remembered me as the hero who stabbed the shit out of Mr. Cullen with a no. 2 pencil. She asked if I remember her. I told her, "Yes. You sat in the second seat in the first row and you were the skinniest kid in the class."

She laughed and I told her I wasn't making fun of her. Looking back, she was the cutest kid in the class. Then she said that I have gotten so pretty. She said I was pretty. That made me blush.

We got to know each other, Wanda and me. She didn't like that I played hooky a lot. She thought it sad that I still got bad grades. She had to pass by my house to go to school, so she started to pick me up. I stopped playing hooky. I went to school every day and, for the first time, I liked it.

My favorite class was English. I realized how much I loved to write. She loved my stories. She took one of my stories and showed it to her teacher. He loved it! He said it was very good. He couldn't believe that such a young woman could write with such depth. He, in turn, showed my story to another and she agreed. They came to my class to meet this talented girl. Me! They said I had a gift. Me!

She saved my life. Wanda helped me with my homework and I helped her with anything she needed to write. My grades improved one hundred percent. I mean, they were amazing. She told me that if I kept applying myself, I could even get a scholarship.

We became the best of friends. I loved being at Wanda's house. It was so heartwarming to see how her parents loved her so. Her parents appreciated their good fortune. Their "born good" child. She came to my house once. I could tell that she felt the coldness. My father eventually said to her, "Girl, go home. Or don't you have a home to go homc to?"

My mother never came out of her room to meet Wanda. I think my mother was ashamed of her swollen eye. My mother was a lovely-faced woman once. Age did not take it away. My father did. Why did she give him so much power? Wanda never came to my house again. I didn't want her to.

One Saturday afternoon when I was at Wanda's house and her parents were out, we lay in her bed reading. Suddenly, she took the book from my hands. She said we should practice kissing so that one day, when we had boyfriends, we would know what to do. I thought, *I don't want a boyfriend.* We kissed, then I suggested while we were at it, we should also practice petting. She agreed. Her breasts felt wonderful and they tasted like strawberry ice cream. Her insides were creamy like the cake batter I dipped my fingers into as a child. I felt a warm flow come out of me and onto my panties. Then I told her I didn't want anyone but her. She said she felt the same way, but she didn't know how to tell me. She cried and said, "We must be weird girls."

I told her no! That she should never feel that way. We cried and laughed and for the first time in my life, I was loved and I could give love, but this strange new wonderful feeling scared me and it didn't. I didn't care and

I did. It was such a euphoric confusion.

It got late. Time slipped away as it always did when I was with her. I knew what awaited me when I got home and I didn't care. The thrill of Wanda's aroma engulfed me. I got home. That's when my happiness came to an end.

(She cries)

I was born bad. Happiness was something fate was not going to allow me to have. I walked in the door. By this time, my reflexes were amazing. I knew my father was behind the door. I ducked and he missed me. He was getting weak from the years of hatred eating away at him. I was young and quick. He missed striking me with that same goddamn belt. I grabbed it in midair. That enraged him. In my head, I heard my classmates laughing. He screamed, "I'll kill you if you don't let go."

I knew at that moment he meant it and it was either him or me. I felt that power come over me again. I knew someone was going to die that night and it was not going to be me. Well, I'm here aren't I? Then he said, "You were with that little whore Wanda, weren't you? I'll fix her wagon if she ever dares to ever show her face around here."

I remembered my Nancy Nurse. I couldn't allow him to do that to Wanda. I looked at the dish rack and I saw a sharp no. 2 pencil. Only it wasn't a pencil. It was a chef knife. The same one he butchered my Nancy Nurse with. I plunged the knife into him, severing the veins in his arm. The second stab plunged into his carotid artery. The third severed his lungs and the final one perforated his heart. *(She laughs)* I found love and lost hate all on the same day.

I sat in the police interrogation room. I didn't say a word. I smiled and felt that power. I knew everyone in that precinct feared and respected me. Like the kids in Mr. Cullen's class, once I showed them not to laugh at me. I thought of how I was going to see Wanda as soon as I got out of there. I was so heartbroken and angry that she didn't come to see me.

When I got out, I found out that she was horrified about what I had done. Her parents feared for her life. They kept me away from her. A restraining order, they call it. An order I got arrested for breaking. I never saw her again. Oh, I know I'll see her again someday and I pity the poor son-of-a-bitch who gets in my way. I love her still. I always will. I will never forget her.

Through the years I got into a lot more trouble because people are notoriously cruel and they make me so angry. It's because of them that I am in this hospital room with no human contact! Treating me as if I were some sort of Hannibal. How dare they! I never ate anyone. I was damned to a fate I had no control over. Now I'm the one who has to pay in this hellhole because I was born bad through no fault of my own. I was simply...chosen.

IN DEFENSE OF STRAIGHT WOMEN

I saw a segment on a Sunday morning show that made me
laugh. It said that Batgirl was going to come out as a
Lesbian. Come on now. Enough of this already. Now, I
love my Lesbian sisters, but enough. Just because a
woman could run faster does not make her a Lesbian. I
think this is an insult to straight women everywhere.
Straight women who have more athletic skills than any
Lesbian I know. I know a straight woman like this.
Anyone would love to have her on their team. Yes, there
are straight women who can build a house, put up kitchen
cabinets, and fix all the plumbing in the house. Yet, I
know some big, brawny butch Lesbians who love baking,
flower arrangements, hate football, can't hammer a nail
into a wall, and will scream like a bitch while jumping
onto a chair because they saw an itty-bitty bug. Not all of
them. I said "some." Let's don't get your feathers ruffled.

This straight woman that I know hates when people
confuse her for a Lesbian. Not because she is homophobic.
She is not. She is all for gay rights. She believes 'in live

and let live' and will march at the head of the line for my – our rights. She's been asked, "So what is wrong with being mistaken for a Lesbian?" She says, "Everything. If that is what you are." I mean, she doesn't go around calling Lesbians straight.

In the movie "A League of Their Own" there is a character called Marla Hooch who could knock a ball clear out of the park. She was not feminine at all. She walked with a rough swagger and spit like a pro. I went with a friend to see that movie and she was appalled when Marla's character fell in love with and married a man. She said Marla's character should have married a woman. Why? This happens to be a straight girl with phenomenal skills. Believe it or not, straight girls can jump.

So, to all those athletic, bad ass, straight women, knock that ball out of the ballpark. More power to you, sister girl. And Batgirl, if you are straight it's okay if you want to date Batman or Robin or any man. You can come out of the closet about being straight. I will still love you. I understand that being straight wasn't a choice. It's not your fault. You were just born that way.

TONKA, BARBIE and ROBERTO

I like fun facts. For example, do you know where the Tonka Truck was originated? A company by the name of Mound Metalcraft was created in 1946 in Mound Minnesota by Lynn Everett Baker. A woman. Her original intent was to manufacture garden implements. The Tonka logo was created by Erling Eklof with the word "Tanka" or "Tonka," which means great or big.

One Christmas, my brother was given a big, beautiful, red and yellow Tonka Truck. It had huge black tires and a steering wheel you could turn with your finger. I thought it was the most beautiful thing I had ever seen. It was so shiny. I can still smell the paint. Funny, there was no fear of toxins in toys back then, yet we survived. Then I opened my gift. It was a Barbie doll. I was so disappointed. There she was with her cat-eye make-up and her beehive nylon hair. All I could think of as I looked down at her was, *nice tits.* Now, I'm not one of those Barbie bashers. I think she's a nice doll for little girls who want one and I don't want Barbie to be abolished just because she's beautiful.

It's just that, Barbie was not for me.

I watched with envy as my brother zoomed that Tonka around the house. I loved the sound of those tires as they rumbled against the linoleum floor and...there I stood, staring down at Barbie's tits.

I was going to get my hands on that Tonka Truck one way or another so I came up with a plan. I waited for my brother to go to sleep. I snuck over by his bed and there was Tonka parked alongside his bed, shining so beautifully by the moonlight that came in through the window. I think that's the first time I fell in love. I quietly took Tonka to my room. Then out of the corner of my eye, I saw Barbie. There she was, sitting on my dresser looking sad because I wouldn't play with her. I felt bad for her because she deserved to be loved too. I took her and I put her in the truck. It was at that moment that I realized how hot a chick in a truck looks.

I fell asleep without returning Tonka to her original spot. Yes, Tonka is a her. Anything that beautiful has to be. I was awakened by my brother's screams when he woke up to discover his truck was missing. He ran into my room. I guess hc knew I was the culprit. He grabbed the truck with Barbie still stuck inside and he yanked her out. I yelled out, "Hey, don't you do that to her!" He ignored me as he also tried to pull out the nylon hair that was stuck in the Tonka.

I loved my brother, but I so envied him being a boy and getting all the cool stuff.

Roberto's Barber Shop…

My mother would take us to Roberto's Barber Shop where my brother got his hair cut. I watched as he hopped onto that chair with all the hardware on it. Roberto would crank up the chair with his foot. I was amazed by the sound of the buzzer that clipped my brother's hair. Then Roberto picked up a bottle of aftershave. The bottle had a picture of a very dapper gentleman wearing a tuxedo. Roberto padded the aftershave on the back of my brother's neck. It smelled so good.

I was excited because I thought I was next. I hopped onto the chair. My mother said, "*Nena baja te de ai! Get down from there. You can't do that You're a girl.*" I turned, saw myself in the mirror, and I did not like what I saw. I had this very long hair that I was not allowed to cut. I begged to, but my father would not allow it. He said it was beautiful. I thought it was ugly. In my childish mind I saw it as a mass of something that was growing out of my head and I wanted to be free from it.

When I got old enough to vote and drink, I walked into Roberto's Barber Shop and sat in that chair. I saw that little girl in the mirror looking back at me, proud of who she grew up to be. Roberto clipped my hair. I loved the way the buzzing tickled my ear. I also bought and now drive a red truck. Remember, Tonka means "great or big." Well she is a great big truck, so I guess I finally got my Tonka, and I named her Barbie.

A STRANGE FEELING

It was only a lump, then suddenly strangers in white masks were cutting away at my beautiful breasts. It was only after that ordeal that I fell in love. Why? Why couldn't this thing called love happen to me when I was whole? When I was....a real woman. Love.

What is this strange feeling? I feel it in my heart. It feels warm. As if butterflies were fluttering around in there. It scares me. I know what it is and I do not want to feel this. How dare she come into my life now? I was so happy without this inconvenience of a feeling. I've heard it said that God has a sense of humor. Well, I'm laughing, sort of.

What is this strange feeling? I can't think. She keeps getting in the way. She is who I want to talk with. To laugh with. To spend all of my time with. I'm a smart woman. I know the sweet words she says to me could be just sympathy, or pity. Or could it be that, well, that maybe she likes me too? I don't know, but I do know this. I do know that I can control this feeling. Can't I?

What is this strange feeling? My mind and my soul want to run to her, but my body just...can't. It's a terrible tug of war within me. You know, I always laughed at people who were confused. Karma sucks.

What is this strange feeling? I don't know. I won't think about it. I just won't think about it and I will make these butterflies go in the direction that I want them to go. *(Laughs)* That is so stupid. Butterflies are sort of like cats. You can't make them go in the direction they don't want.

Or maybe this is a phase and in time I won't like her. Yes, that's it! In time, this strange feeling will turn into my realizing that I only liked her as a friend and then I can go back to not feeling this...wonderful feeling. Then I can go back to when I was....happy. This inconvenience of a feeling will go away. It will, really. Or will it?

WOMAN, PUERTO RICAN, AND LESBIAN

Woman, Puerto Rican, and Lesbian. Someone once said to me, "Wow, that's three strikes against you."

When I came out to my mother so many years ago, she cried. She held her head and her heart. I didn't know if she was going to have a faint or have a heart attack or both. She said, "I would rather you had told me you were a whore in the street than to tell me you are that." She said, "I'll never be able to show my face again, I'm so ashamed. What have I done that was so bad that God felt he had to punish me with a child like you?"

A child like me. A child like that. She couldn't even say the word. She was a good woman, my mother, but those were different times and having a Lesbian daughter was a fate worse than death and a disgrace to my people.

I also came out to my favorite aunt. She was a cool aunt and I thought she would understand because her best friend was a gay man. She didn't understand. She said,

"What do you mean? What is wrong with you? You can't do that. I don't understand. We are Puerto Ricans and we don't do that."

I thought, what could I do? How could I change this? I knew I couldn't change it overnight, but I had to do something, start somewhere, make a difference and leave my mark. So I decided to fight back. I was young and full of anger and hope. I marched with the Harvey Milks and against the Anita Bryants. I carried my sign in protest, raised my fist in the air, and marched alongside my gay brothers and sisters for justice. Hell, it was the 1970's. The Aura, the electricity of the Stonewall riots was still in the air. In the streets, we were beaten and spit at. Undercover police were arresting same sex couples for dancing too close to each other. We were shunned by our families. Fired and forbidden to teach our children in public schools. We had to keep that closet door shut tight, not allowing even a sliver of light to slip through the cracks, but like a rubber band pulled to a point where it could stretch no more, we snapped and kicked down that closet door with a vengeance because we had had enough. We were proud and we ignited a blazing trail that was seen all over the world.

I was there. Now here I am so many years later. Joyous of how free the young, gay generation gets to enjoy the fruits of our fight. I just hope they know. Appreciate our history. Know of the blood spilled in the streets and of the lives lost, but not in vain because we are now able to marry, to work, to teach, to love. It's sad those that sacrificed their lives never got to see it. I'm so blessed that I did. Why did I survive? I don't know. Maybe so that I could be here at this very moment? I don't know. Yes, I was kicked and spit on, and this is going to sound strange, but this...is just a body and it was all worth it.

Woman, Puerto Rican, and Lesbian? Hell yeah

PARK BENCH

(Emily enters carrying groceries and a bottle of champagne. She sits. She picks up the champagne. She is sad. Enter Allen. Sits and reads his newspaper. Emily looks at him. She recognizes him as someone she often sees in the park.)

EMILY

Good morning. Nice to see you again.

ALLEN

Good morning. Same here. I thought I recognized you.

EMILY

Yes. I usually sit over there.
(She knocks her umbrella off of the bench. Allen picks it up.)

EMILY

Thank you. You're a gentleman.

(ALLEN laughs)

EMILY

What?

ALLEN

My wife said that to me when we met. She dropped her
purse. I picked it up and she called me a gentlemen.

(EMILY *laughs*)

ALLEN

What?

EMILY

That's what attracted me to my husband. Such a
gentleman.

ALLEN

It looks like you're going to prepare quite some dinner.

EMILY

All my husband's favorites. Steak, baked potato with
butter, vegetable, and a salad.

ALLEN

And champagne. Celebrating something special?

EMILY
(Sad)

An anniversary.

ALLEN

Nice. I'm sure your husband will be very pleased.

EMILY

My husband passed away five years ago.

ALLEN
(Looks confused)

Ha?

EMILY

No, no. Let me explain. You're going to think I'm off my rocker. You see, every year on the anniversary of my husband's death, which is today, I prepare all of his favorites. It's just something I do. It makes me feel as if he were with me. Oh, hell, I guess I am off my rocker. I can't believe I'm telling you this.

ALLEN

It's alright. Don't apologize. *(BEAT)* My wife made the best broiled salmon. She also used butter and just the right amount of lemon. It was like biting into a piece of heaven.

EMILY

You said "made." She doesn't prepare it anymore?

ALLEN

No. My wife passed away six years, three months, two weeks, and four days ago today.

EMILY

Wow! You count. I cook. Strange what grief can do.

ALLEN

True. *(Goes back to reading his paper then looks back at Emily.)* Can I ask you something?

EMILY

Sure.

ALLEN

Never mind.

EMILY

Oh no. You can't do that. Now you have to ask me or I'll lose sleep wondering what the question was.

ALLEN

Do people ever say to you, or do you ever get tired of hearing people say, "Move on. It's been so many years. It's time to move on with your life?"

EMILY

Yes. I've heard this one: "Maybe you should get a dog or a cat or a fish."

ALLEN

Yes! Or how about this one: "You'll meet someone when you least expect it. Maybe in the supermarket or on a plane or on a train." The list goes on. I mean, what do they think? That someone will just fall from the sky and land right next to me?

EMILY

Yeah, right. It's the people who love us who give us this advice. They don't want to see us grieve anymore because it will make them feel better. They want to see us happy again, bless their souls.

ALLEN

You're right. They love us and mean well.

EMILY

They just don't understand. I've had the love of my life, but I'm afraid.

ALLEN

How do you mean?

EMILY

I feel the memories are slowly fading. I feel like I'm starting to reach a point where I no longer smell the breakfast he prepared for me every morning or hear him brushing his teeth or hear him say that...he loves me, and that scares me.

ALLEN

I'm sorry. I didn't mean to...

EMILY

It's okay. I'm just being silly.

ALLEN

No you're not. I feel the same way on the anniversary or my wife's...

EMILY

I'm sorry. Oh! I am being such a wet blanket.

ALLEN

You're not being a wet blanket. *(Sigh)* It actually feels good to talk about this to someone who understands.

EMILY

And you are being very kind to a complete stranger.

ALLEN

So, I'm kind and a gentleman. You're good for my ego. I should sit next to you more often.

EMILY

Yes, you should.

(BEAT)

ALLEN

Strangers, I've always depended...

BOTH

...on the kindness of strangers. *(Looks at each other, points.)* "Street Car Named Desire!"

EMILY

My husband loved that movie. He was a huge classic movie fan.

ALLEN

This is too coincidental. So was my wife. As a matter of fact, on our first date we went to see Street Car at the old Paramount Theatre.

EMILY

My husband and I saw Street Car the first time I went to his apartment. I mean the first time we...I mean...We saw it on the Turner Classic Movie channel.

ALLEN

Giving up a little too much information there.

EMILY

(Is embarrassed but continues.)

I never knew about the Classic Movie channel before I met my husband.

ALLEN

Before Street Car, all I ever knew about Vivien Leigh was "Gone with the Wind." She was amazing as Blanche in Street Car and as Cleopatra in "Cesar and Cleopatra." The costumes she wore in that movie...wow!

EMILY

Claude Rains was also in Cesar and Cleopatra. I had never

heard of him before that, but his performance…I just fell in love with him. My favorite was his role in the movie "Mr. Skeffington."

ALLEN

Didn't Bette Davis play the role of his wife in that movie?

EMILY

Yes she did! Very good! I am impressed. Did you know that Claude and Bette became very good friends, lifelong friends?

ALLEN

Yes I did.

EMILY

Yeah.

(BEAT)

ALLEN

It looks like it's going to rain.

EMILY

Claude.

ALLEN

What?

EMILY

We were talking about Claude Rains and you said, "It looks like it's going to rain," so I said, "Claude." Never mind. I was trying to be funny.

ALLEN

Yes, I get it. Claude Rains.

EMILY

Yeah

ALLEN

Yeah.

EMILY

If it does rain, I've got my umbrella. *(BEAT)* The old Paramount Theatre. I haven't been there since I was a child.

ALLEN

They're still showing the classics every third Friday of the month. That would be…tomorrow.
      (ALLEN stands, takes a few steps towards the

audience, and speaks to them.)
I am such an idiot! Why did I say that? She probably thinks I'm trying to ask her to go to the movies with me. I'm not. I wouldn't mind. Damnit! It was just conversation. I should just read my paper and keep my big mouth shut.
(He sits. They look at each other and smile. He picks up his paper and starts to read. He looks at EMILY when she starts to speak.)

EMILY

I would love to see a movie there again, someday. I just don't like to go to the movies alone.
(She stands and takes a few steps towards the audience.)
Shit! He probably thinks I'm hinting for him to take me to the movies. I'm not! I wouldn't mind. He's so cute and kind. Agh! I feel like such an idiot.
(She sits.)

ALLEN

The movie starts at eight.

EMILY

What?

ALLEN

The movie. At the Paramount. It starts at eight in the evening.

EMILY

Really? I think I'll go. I need to treat myself.

ALLEN

Me too.

EMILY

Hey, if I run into you, I'll buy you a popcorn.

ALLEN

I'll buy you a box of Raisinettes. Do they still make Raisinettes?

EMILY

Good question.

ALLEN

You know, since we're both going to be there, why don't we just meet? To keep each other company. I mean, we'll just be sitting together like here, on this bench, except there will be a movie screen in front of us.

EMILY

Yes, like sitting here on this bench, but with comfy seats.

ALLEN

And walls.

EMILY

And a roof, in case it rains.

BOTH

Claude!

(They laugh)

EMILY

Well, I've got to go.

(She stands and grabs her purse.)

ALLEN

Yes, sure. I understand. You have a lot of cooking to do.

EMILY

Excuse me?

ALLEN

(Stands and helps her with the grocery bag.)

You have a lot of cooking to do.

EMILY

Oh...yes. That's right. Thank you.
(She takes the bag and starts to walk away.)

ALLEN

Excuse me.

EMILY
(Quickly turns.)

Yes?

ALLEN

My name is Allen.

EMILY

I'm Emily.

ALLEN

Emily. Pretty name.

EMILY

Thank you...Allen.
(EMILY, again, turns to walk away.)

ALLEN

Excuse me, Emily?

EMILY

Yes?

ALLEN

I will be there tomorrow, at the Paramount. 8:00 o' clock.

EMILY

Me too.

(ALLEN sits. EMILY starts to walk away. She stops, looks up, turns to look at ALLEN. Exit EMILY)

(ALLEN looks up, thinking of his wife. He notices the handkerchief. He picks it up, smiles as he wipes his eyes. He starts to walk away, looks back at the bench, and looks up again. Exit ALLEN)

IT'S NOT A JOB

I was standing on the platform of the subway waiting for the number two train to The Bronx. There were three young women standing beside me. One of them was obviously going to have a baby. I was shocked at how unsupportive her friends were. I heard one of them say, "Welcome to the hardest job in the world." The other friend said, "Sure is and you don't get paid for it either."

That poor girl. I saw her face go from pure excitement to hurt from their reaction. I wanted to go over to her and say, "No. That's not true. I lived through it and I am now a grandmother and I loved every minute of it."

The hardest job in the world? Don't say that to a young woman who is about to have a baby. First of all, it's not a job, but she will get paid with a lifetime of wonderful memories. Don't discourage her.

Tell her that she has been given the highest of all blessings. Tell her that she has just been sat upon a throne and on her head has been placed a most priceless crown. A crown dripping with the most flawless of jewels. Tell her that, with that crown, comes a long, flowing cape made of the finest velvet to protect her and keep her warm throughout this life that she has been blessed with. Don't discourage her.

Tell her that the first tooth that shines through will be more priceless than any pearl and the sound of that child's voice the first time that child says "mama" cannot be described. Tell her you will envy the day she sees her child take that first step. That you will envy the tear she will shed on her child's first day of school, the first play, birthday party, and graduation. Don't discourage her.

Tell her that there will be hardships, but to be patient and wait for the blessings that will flow from them and that there will always, always be a light at the end of the tunnel. Don't discourage her.

Tell her, and this is the most important – if you forget anything don't let it be this – you tell her that one day when she gets to add jewels to that crown and becomes a GRANDMOTHER, she will be most grateful to have been blessed with more than just a mere job.

AN INTERESTING CONVERSATION

I had a very interesting conversation with a woman from Greece. She said something that enlightened me. She said that only the people from the island of Lesbos are Lesbians. People from Italy are Italian, people from Puerto Rico are Puerto Ricans, and so on. She informed me that this Eastern Mediterranean paradise was one of the cradles of mankind. All the way back to the Homo Sapiens, Neanderthals, and Homo Erectus. In the fifteenth century, the Greeks from Mycenae made their appearance in Lesbos and neighboring Asia Minor. These were the times of the Trojan War. Her brain was really turning, really turning me on.

Anyway, Lesbos, Homo Sapiens, Homo Erectus, and Trojan. I'm seeing a connection here. Her point was, only people from Lesbos are Lesbians. The men are Lesbians, the straight women are Lesbians, and all the little children are Lesbians. I asked what homosexual women in Lesbos are called. She said, "homosexual" or "gay." I don't know how true that is, but that's what she said. Then we talked about the word "homosexual" and why we feel we have to sugarcoat the word. Is it because the word is too real? Like when society once said "with child" instead of "pregnant?"

I went home, curious. I looked up the word homosexual. In a real dictionary. The one with the red cover because I wanted to get it right. It said, "Homosexual: Sexual desire, behavior toward a person, or persons, of one's own sex."

Then I remembered she mentioned the word "gay." Decades ago, the word "gay" did not mean homosexual. It meant beyond happiness. So I go back to the dictionary and it said, "GAY: Joyous mood. Bright or showy. Happy or light hearted mood. A lightness of heart or liveliness of mood that is openly manifested." Okay. I have to agree with that, but – and here is the big but – I don't feel happy and joyous and lively all the time. So, when I'm cranky or ill- humored, I am not gay. I am not from The Island of Lesbos, so I am, technically, not a Lesbian, but according to the Webster's Dictionary I do fit the description of a homosexual.

I will always remember this very interesting conversation I had with this very lovely women from Greece and know that what I *truly* am is a homosexual.

MILK and ORANGE JUICE

Gay activist and community leader Harvey Milk made history. He was one of the first openly gay officials, not only in California, but in the United States. Milk was born in Woodmere, New York on May 22, 1930. Raised in a small, middle-class, Jewish family, he was one of two boys. His parents were William and Minerva Milk. He was a well-liked student. He played football and sang opera at Bay Shore High School. In 1951, he joined the U.S. Navy as a diving instructor at a base in San Diego California during the Korean War. He was discharged in 1955 and moved back to New York where he worked as a public school teacher, production associate for famous Broadway shows, stock analyst, and Wall Street banker. He never seemed to be content in one place. Milk became very much a part of the "in" crowd and befriended gay radicals in the infamous Greenwich Village.

In 1972 he moved to San Francisco California. He opened a camera shop on Castro Street in the heart of the city's gay community. Milk stayed quiet about his personal life. As Castro Camera became a neighborhood center, Milk found his voice as a leader and activist. In 1973 he declared his candidacy for a position on San Francisco's Board of Supervisors. Milk lost that election, but this did not deter him. He tried again two years later. Milk became a political force and outspoken leader in the gay community with political connections that included San Francisco Mayor George Mascone, Assembly Speaker Willie Brown, and future U.S. Senator Dianne Feinstein.

In 1977 Milk was affectionately known as "The Mayor of Castro Street" and won a seat on the San Francisco City-County Board. He was inaugurated on January 9, 1978. The first openly gay officer as well as one of the first openly gay individuals to be elected to office, Milk fought for a variety of issues, from child care to housing to a civil police review board and the pooper-scooper law.

Many psychiatrists still considered homosexuality a mental illness. Mayor Mascone, who was a supporter of gay rights, abolished the anti-sodomy law. Mascone appointed several gay and lesbians to high profile positions within San Francisco. On the other side, Supervisor Dan White was appalled by what he perceived as a breakdown in mortality, traditional values, and growing tolerance of homosexuality. He went head on with liberal Harvey Milk on policy issues. White resigned from the board, then subsequently changed his mind and asked Mascone to reassign him. Mascone refused and was encouraged by Milk to fill White's spot with a more liberal board member. This was a devastating blow for White. White was convinced that men like Mascone were driving the city downhill.

On November 27, 1978, White entered City Hall with a loaded 38 revolver. He passed by the metal detectors by entering through a basement window left open for ventilation. His first stop was the mayor's office where the men were heard arguing. They moved to a private room where the men could not be heard. Mascone again refused to re-appoint White. White shot the mayor twice in the chest, and twice in the head. White then went down the corridor to Milk's office and shot Milk twice in the chest, once in the back, and twice in the head.

ORANGE JUICE

Anita Bryant was born on March 25, 1940. A Miss America runner-up who became the spokeswoman for Tropicana Orange Juice, turned anti-gay campaigner in the late 1970's, Bryant condemned homosexuality as immoral and against God's laws. In 1977 Bryant campaigned to repeal a Miami ordinance banning anti-gay discrimination. She started the organization, "Save Our Children." Bryant claimed that gays were converting our children to homosexuality. Then she turned her sights on Florida adoption laws. Since homosexuals cannot reproduce, Bryant reasoned that homosexuals would adopt children to recruit and freshen their ranks. Bryant convinced the Florida legislators to pass a law to entirely bar homosexuals from adopting children. Because of Bryant's negative views on homosexuality and campaigning against gay rights, she was targeted by gay rights activists in a boycott of the orange juice industry. She eventually lost her job as spokeswoman due to this and she was widely condemned as a homophobe which resulted in the ending of her entertainment career. More than two and a half decades later, Miami finally passed an anti-gay bias ordinance and Anita Bryant slipped into obscurity.

These are some of Anita Bryant's famous quotes:

- "I love homosexuals. It's the sin of homosexuality I hate."
- After being pied in the face by a gay protestor during a press conference, she said, "At least it was a fruit pie."

- "Had I gone my own way and not gotten to know God or accept him in my life, I think I would have been a very belligerent individual full of hate and bitterness."
- "If gays are granted rights, next we'll have to give rights to prostitutes, people who sleep with Saint Bernard's, and nail biters."

LOVE IS FOREVER
A one man monologue

He told me that he will stop loving me when he closes his eyes forever. Well, that's not long enough. You see, after you close your eyes forever, there is eternity and that is how long love lasts.

I love you to the moon and back and as far as all the stars above. Well, that's not far enough. That's right, because all of the above could never go as far as love can reach. We do not love our children from the day they are born. No. We loved our children the day the earth itself was born because that is the day that loving your child was destined and cast in stone.

There is a song that says "Gibraltar will crumble, it's only made of clay, but our love is here to stay." Truer words have never been written. Gibraltar may crumble someday and when it does, love will look down on it and say, "Look at you, all crumpled, but I am love and I am here to stay."